THE

IT awok[e] ___ ___ ___ ___
ing, trees l___, birds screaming, animals running,
fire snapping and snarling both inside and out.

IT dragged ITself from the wreckage of ITs craft
and waited for ITs vision to clear.

And when it had, IT knew that IT had reached ITs
destination.

IT knew that soon, very soon, the killing would
begin.

" 'Ey, Pancho," IT said to ITself in clear delight,
"go saddle the horses. We ride at dawn!"

KENT MONTANA AND THE REALLY UGLY THING FROM MARS

LIONEL FENN

ACE BOOKS, NEW YORK

This book is an Ace original edition,
and has never been previously published.

KENT MONTANA
AND THE REALLY UGLY THING FROM MARS

An Ace Book/published by arrangement with
the author

PRINTING HISTORY
Ace edition/August 1990

ISBN: 0-441-43535-1

Ace Books are published by The Berkley Publishing Group,
200 Madison Avenue, New York, New York 10016.
The name ''ACE'' and the ''A'' logo
are trademarks belonging to Charter Communications, Inc.

PRINTED IN THE UNITED STATES OF AMERICA

10 9 8 7 6 5 4 3 2 1

There is nothing quite so terrible as
a battle with the unknown;

There is nothing quite so wonderful as
a battle with the unknown;

There is nothing quite so wonderful and terrible as
a really bad movie when you don't have anything else
to do on a rainy day and your dog has fleas.

—Geoffrey Marsh
(who, if he didn't say it,
should have, because he's my
brother and I asked him to)

KENT MONTANA AND THE REALLY UGLY THING FROM MARS

–I–

The Players

◆ 1 ◆

Kent Montana, whose real last name was known only to his mother, his sister, and a few dozen family retainers who didn't give a damn one way or the other as long as their pensions and positions were intact if not secure, decided after much painful deliberation that if he was going to abandon his acting career, and thus engage in the wanton destruction of a life-long dream, he ought to do it in such a way that he could change his mind without too much embarrassment and humiliation in case things suddenly looked up.

A courageous, declarative notice in the *Times* was therefore probably out of the question.

So was firing his agent.

Otherwise it would be just his luck that, at the very moment of his theatrical demise, a breathless messenger would come to his apartment door bearing the script he'd been waiting for all his life. It would be chock-full of pithy epigrams, witty bon mots, and such convivial conversation that his name, and no other, would have to be scribbled next to the lead; it would be so brilliant that Noel Coward would leave his grave in order to praise and direct it; it would be so perfect that even his mother would have to quit bitching about his profession and stop trying to sell the family estate and winery on a remote and unnamed Hebrides Isle.

And so, on a warm humid night filled with stars and promise and the scent of pine from the nearby forest, as he stood in a tartan bathrobe on the fifth-floor terrace of his Gander

3

Pond, New Jersey, high-rise condominium, he debated the morality of what he was about to do, and concluded that morality would only confuse him into indecision.

A puzzlement; a dilemma.

With a slight frown, he braced himself against the sturdy ironwork railing and peered down, rubbing his squared jaw thoughtfully, then scratching through an embarrassing abundance of ginger hair, then backing up hastily when a silver ice bucket plummeted from the terrace directly above his, accompanied by the delighted laughter of a woman and the guffaws of her male companion.

He glared upward.

He sighed.

He tried to ignore the subsequent muffled murmurings and coy gigglings and sophisticated clinks of crystal champagne glasses; he definitely paid no attention to the terrace immediately below, from which wafted heavy breathing, more than a few healthy groans, one or two slaps of flesh against slick flesh, and the astonished yowl of an evidently uninvited cat.

Life goes on without me, he reflected morosely, and he approached the railing again, albeit somewhat warily, as he contemplated the parking lot, in hopes that its dark expanse might give him a clue of how to cleverly weasel his perhaps decision without forcing a definite commitment.

Or at least figure out another way to make a living before his mother found out and bribed a judge to have him declared missing, presumed dead.

The trouble was, Gander Pond—which had no pond at all, or even an occasional clogged storm drain—was in the geographic middle of just about nowhere in particular. It was a small and tidy community intimately surrounded by high hills and dense forest, sustained by summer tourism, autumn hunting, and spring fishing, and the several score idiots who had purchased condominiums in the Gander Palace, at ten stories and shaped like a pyramid, the second tallest structure in the county. He had come here himself because the price was right, his Manhattan landlord was a prick who demanded timely rent, and the telephone service here was erratic, thus permitting him to hang up on his mother without feeling laden with too much guilt about severing a transatlantic call.

I am adrift, he thought miserably, staring at the woodland

that began immediately where the parking lot ended; I am at sea, I am marooned, I am—

A jerk, he was told.

Bosh! I am an artist, he responded heatedly.

You are a soon-to-be-impoverished Scottish-born actor who was canned from *Passions and Power* because you kept rewriting the script for relevance and more airtime. Jesus, it was only a soap drama, for god's sake.

Daytime drama, he corrected huffily, and the scripts—if you can call them that—made me look and sound like a complete buffoon, a jester, a stereotypical English butler without a brain in his head.

You *were* an English butler.

Yeah, well . . .

The audible writhings below were deftly overlaid by spicy salsa with a clear New Orleans beat; above, the couple in the penthouse had taken to playing obscure Beethoven on her imported steel wind chimes.

And in the summer sky, the stars multiplied in cosmic arithmetic, making him feel inordinately small, uncomfortably untalented, and rather unsuited to standing naked beneath a bathrobe in rural New Jersey.

One of the stars moved.

He contemplated it for a second, then declared to the faceless moon, "Life is like a soufflé—it takes forever to get it right, and once you get it in the oven, someone slams the door and the whole thing falls flat."

The cat yowled.

"Quite right," he agreed without hesitation. "Drivel. Utter drivel."

The salsa segued into reggae.

The wind chimes pinged a requiem.

But on his own modest pied-à-terre there was nothing but dismal silence. The telephone didn't ring, the doorbell didn't buzz, and the fact that it was a shade past ten o'clock on the fifth day of August didn't faze him at all. Opportunity's call knew no time, no date, no barrier to delivery. It had also forgotten where the hell he lived, and if it didn't remember soon, the bank was going to foreclose and toss him out of here on his aristocratic ass.

A prolonged sigh just to the left of, and slightly behind,

melodramatic, and he focused once more on the slow-moving mysterious light, located now high above Gander Mountain to the east. A satellite, he concluded in semidisinterest, chin cupped in one hand, left foot unconsciously tapping out the rhythm of the music below, which was now accompanied by the shrieks of a woman either having one hell of a good time or being dismembered cell by cell.

He changed his mind about the satellite theory when the light abruptly swerved left, hovered for several seconds, then swerved back the way it had come.

Ah. Not an uncaring electronic baseball at all, but undoubtedly a lost pilot. A solitary soul in the blackness of night, searching for his homeland amid the illuminated garden of humanity below.

A kindred, if somewhat distant, spirit.

Then it abruptly reversed direction yet again, and he immediately calculated the angle of its apparent steep descent, checked his building, and decided he was safe.

But what in the long run would it matter if the airplane did strike him? Who would miss him? Who would care? Who would mourn his splattered loss?

Who, indeed, Kent? Who indeed?

Certainly not his older sister, who had precipitously married an American steelworker twelve years ago and had been instrumental in bringing him over to this benighted country in the first place; she barely knew he was alive and kept calling him Dakota. Definitely not his mother, who was still trying to figure out a way to sue him for his title so that she could sell the estate and build a modest cottage in Majorca. And without question not the United States Immigration Service, who had already informed him that his time was up, his welcome mat snatched away, and if he wasn't out of the country in ninety days, his lordship was going to find himself checked in with the grubby peasants of some Bastille or other.

"Was there anyone," he whispered to the night-shrouded mountain, "so troubled as I? Was there anyone so besieged, so beleaguered, so becalmed? Am I truly star-crossed, condemned, the bastard son of Fate? Shall I—"

Another bucket fell.

A windshield shattered a few seconds later.

He didn't look. He wasn't worried. He knew it wasn't his

automobile, because that had been mercifully parked, as it always was, in the farthest, darkest corner of the lot. Half the time he couldn't find it; and when he did, half the time he changed his mind about getting in. It was a rather unique vehicle, and the less he was seen in it, the better he felt it was for his tottering image as a civilized human being.

Reggae became Glenn Miller.

The airplane shifted oddly again, and this time he realized that its running lights weren't blinking, nor were they of a color he usually saw on such lofty craft. Though it was still some distance away, the light seemed almost purple in nature. Refraction or reflection, he decided; no plane had purple lights. That would be silly.

Glenn Miller became a wandering jazz sonnet blessedly cut off in mid-improvisation, and the resulting silence relieved him as the night closed in. Only the leaves in the trees, the night birds, a distant siren.

Dying, he decided, would be stupid.

A voice called, "Kent, you up there?" very softly.

Gathering his robe about him and making a quick check above, he leaned over as far as he dared. There, below, was a black-haired, dusky-skinned, wide-eyed face looking back at him. He smiled. She smiled back and winked.

"You thought I was fooling around, right?"

He shook his head immediately. "Never crossed my mind."

"Liar."

He couldn't help but grin.

She brandished a black plastic rectangle. "Tape," she explained, grinning back. "A little porn for my party."

He believed her. Chita Juarel was a woman whose life-style continually befuddled him. Though currently an expert waitress at Sophia Chong's Pagoda on Main Street's Restaurant Row, she had also been in the chorus lines of three successful Broadway shows, a logger in Oregon, a Miami fortune-teller, and a bartender in two Atlantic City casinos. She had come to Gander Pond, to live in Gander Palace at the foot of Gander Mountain, in order to contemplate the rest of her life and, he was positive, make his life miserable.

When she eased a bit farther out over her railing, he knew it was so—delicate bare shoulders gleamed in the golden light from her apartment, and he had no doubt that the gleam didn't stop with the top of her cleavage. Taunting. Teasing. Yet she thus far had refused to date him. She had a thing, she'd once told him, against men raised in convents. Irrational, to be sure, but perhaps she'd get over it, one of these days.

"So what are you doing?" she asked.

It was disconcerting, looking down at a face looking up at him. He blinked several times, lifted one foot for balance, checked for buckets again.

"Watching that plane," he said at last, pointing.

She twisted around to look. Her slender back was bare. "That one?" She pointed.

"Which one?"

"Over there."

"That one?"

"Yes."

"No, that one," he said, pointing. "Over that way, by the mountain."

"Oh. That one."

"It's purple."

"There are no purple lights on planes."

"It looks purple to me."

"Looks purple to me too."

"Then it's purple." It was also growing larger. "I think it's coming this way."

Chita hunched her shoulders; the muscles rippled and flowed and made him wonder if she ever bench-pressed her dates. "I don't hear nothing. A plane comes, you're supposed to hear something."

"It's too far away to hear anything."

She shrugged and glanced over her shoulder. "You want to come down, join the party?"

His smile was weak. "I'm not terribly good at group parties."

"That's okay. It's only me."

He could feel it then, without warning—the earth trembling, the building vibrating, all of it a sure sign that his life was about to change without benefit of script. It made the night air catch in his lungs; it made his heart race around the final turn; it made him grip the railing fiercely just as Chita yelled and the earth trembled and the building vibrated and the air filled with a stark purple light that blinded him and a guttural roar that deafened him, and before he could move, an ice bucket bounced off his skull and sent him reeling to the floor.

'Tis nothing, he thought as his forehead struck the terrace; 'tis nothing, m'lord, what the hell, I'm just dying.

John Smith hated stars, the moon in any phase, and just about everything else that made Gander Pond and its environs such a delight for those who didn't have to live there. Besides, seeing the universe spread so obliquely above him only made him sneeze. This reaction, he knew, was in part an automatic psychological repercussion to the slings and arrows that daily pelted and punctured his ass.

But that wasn't the sad part.

The sad part was, he could have been a great man. He knew it without question. All the opportunities had been there, he certainly had the requisite brains, and there was no question but that his family had the influence.

The problem was his name.

Every time he opened his mouth to give it, he got The Look.

The Look that said, *sure it is, and I'm Pocahontas*; The Look that dared him with a knowing sneer to write it on the guest register with a bold hand and a straight face; The Look that suggested that if he didn't have a better imagination than that, he should easily be able to find substantial work in television news.

The Look that told him he was a walking vaudeville joke.

Yet he had never been able to bring himself to change it. Not only was his father considerably larger than he, but his mother had refined her performances of maternal martyrdom to such an exquisite degree that simply waking up in the morning as a teenager had often made him wish he could cut his throat and save her the trouble.

The funeral would have been spectacular.

A sigh, then, for fortunes lost and power untapped and women unimpressed as he scuttled across Main Street and ducked expertly into the alley where he knew he would find the most succulent pickings from the two restaurants that shared it.

A cooling breeze touched his face.

The sound of distant music from Marcello's Bar and Dance Lounge down the street filled the humid night.

And John wiped his lips and cleared his throat, preparing himself for dinner.

It hadn't always been this way, of course. The bonds his self-evident demonic christening had lashed about him hadn't always thwarted his desires. But times changed. Robber barons and financial empires required names that sounded French, or Dutch, or German; pure American was out because it raised too many suspicions about the competency of one's education. And soon after he graduated from college, he was forced out of his home and his job in the family business.

And once the bank account was gone, he was forced into the streets.

His father subsequently disowned him in a letter posted to General Delivery; his mother stoked herself into operatic recriminations; and his siblings, with names like Lance and Georgette and Samantha, took over the reins of the company without so much as a by-your-leave or vice-presidency nod in his direction.

"Honestly," his sister told him the last time they met, "do you really think Peru is going to buy bonds from a guy named Smith? Get serious, John."

Get serious indeed.

And so it was that he, scion and black sheep, inexorably slipped through the cracks of humanity's floorboards until he was one with and of the basement.

It was a bitch, and soon enough he had left his beloved Long Island for the friendlier climes of rural New Jersey, where living in the woods was a sign of manliness, not a nut; where tourists on vacation gave him money so they could soothe their guilt and relax; where the hills protected him and the forests gave him shelter.

Until the end of the first summer, when a raccoon nearly tore his arm off and a bobcat scared him shitless.

Gander Pond had been his next stop—compact and clean and tolerant of its bums.

Here at last he had found peace.

Here at last he had found his harbor.

Here at last he had discovered the sublime and near orgasmic difference between fresh acorns and discarded macadamias.

Carefully then, so as not to expose his threadbare yellow cotton shirt to the disgusting yet mouth-watering display of nocturnal rubbish, he closed his threadbare tweed topcoat over his scrawny chest with one hand, while the other expertly and swiftly made its way through the squadron of garbage cans that lined the soiled brick walls.

Ten minutes later he snorted his disgust—people were eating well tonight, the bastards, which meant he wouldn't. And there wasn't a hell of a lot of nourishment in broken-open fortune cookies and ribs that were more spare than his.

It looked as if he was going to have to beg.

He winced.

It was so demeaning, so lower-class.

He was rather lucky he was good at it or he would have starved years ago.

One last pass provided no miracles, so, drawing himself up, he did his best to wipe the grime from his stubbled face, the soot from his clothes, the expression of superiority that clung to his lips like twin orange rinds. Then he sniffed, brushed back his hair with both hands, and stepped out of the alley.

Straight into the hands of Officer Lucian Twiller.

"Jesus," Twiller said, averting his face, wrinkling his pug nose, "you stink, John."

Diplomacy rampant in his veins, John said nothing. Twiller was second-in-command on the Gander Pond police force, an English bulldog with bandy legs and a slobber to match. His dark blue uniform strained across muscles he worked on every day, and his cap, with more braid than a Latin American dictator's, had a beak so highly polished he often dropped it to the pavement to check under pedestrian dresses to search for contraband. He was also primary deacon of the Holy Spirit Today Tabernacle Society, and thus bound by Scripture to help the helpless, comfort the comfortless, stiff the poor.

"Christ, when was the last time you had a bath?"

John still held his peace. He knew what was coming. Twiller would offer him a friendly ride out of town, to the shack in the woods where John made his home. The policeman would slip him a few dollars, stop to pick up a sandwich or two at Kettle's Late Shack along the way, quote him a few symbolic yet relevant verses from the glove compartment Bible, then whomp him upside the head once or twice just to prove he was serious about upholding the law.

It was a familiar routine.

"C'mon, pal, let's get you something decent to eat and get you home."

John felt a headache coming on.

"Okay?" the policeman asked, voice hoarse with concern. "What do you say, John? Let's let these good citizens alone and get you into bed."

The street was deserted.

John glanced over his shoulder at the ungrateful garbage, and nodded wearily. What the hell. What were a few lumps when tuna fish was in the offing?

The patrol car was sleek and new, and air-conditioned so powerfully that he began to shiver as soon as he was settled. Yet he didn't complain; he only grunted at the earnest biblical admonitions Twiller sent his way, shrugged at the heartfelt exhortations to stop mooching and get a job, and suggested someone hold the mayo when Twiller pulled up at Kettle's Late Shack Diner just east of town.

Twiller scowled. "Charity," he admonished, "is not something to make demands upon, John. It comes from the heart, the soul, and if you don't have the mayo, all the tuna fish falls apart."

John nodded contritely.

"Don't move."

"I won't."

Twiller handcuffed him to a stainless-steel rail on the dashboard.

"Hey, I said I wasn't going to move!"

"Pilgrim," the policeman said through the window, "life's a bash and then you dash."

John watched him waddle authoritatively into the diner, then picked at his nails as he sought to recall which one of the saints had said that. He had gotten as far as Saint Kevin the Dumb when Twiller returned, unlocked the handcuffs, and dropped a sandwich in his lap.

"Thank you," said John, mustering as much humble as he could without salivating.

"You're welcome. God loves you."

"Yes."

Twiller pulled out of the parking lot and onto the road. "He does, John, and don't you ever forget it."

"I shan't."

Twiller whomped him. "God don't like no funny talk."

John would have replied had he the chance. However, he was instantly reduced to a startled gasp when a sudden, painfully bright purple light washed over the car, followed instantly by a guttural thunderclap that made him clamp his hands to his ears, not caring about the tuna fish that ran down his cheeks.

"Jesus H!" Twiller shrieked as he slammed both feet on the brakes and tried not to hit the trees. "God Almighty, what the hell was that?"

It was widely believed among the locals in Gander Pond that if Sophia Chong looked any more Italian, she'd be the Bay of Naples. As it was, her black hair, her olive skin, her husky size, her faint but seductive mustache, and the volume of her baritone voice often puzzled many of her regular customers, wondering why a woman like this was in a place like this in a town like this.

Sophia didn't care.

The Pagoda was one of the most popular establishments in Gander Pond outside the overpriced hotels down the street. The front of the large restaurant contained only small tables, from which diners could enjoy the endless parade of other tourists on Main Street; the middle section, separated from the front and back thirds by six-foot-long fern-filled teak planters extending from either wall, contained both booths and tables, from which diners could enjoy the Genghis Khan and Bruce Lee murals painted by her nephew; the third section contained only booths, the floor space between occupied by a bountiful smorgasbord table that contained fifteen kinds of pasta, fourteen exotic sauces, thirteen fish dishes, and a bottle of house wine.

Such a munificent array was offset only by the three-foot

red and gold embossed menus in Chinese and Italian which the other diners studied.

It was her clear idea of heaven.

Yet, at the same time, she knew that none of it would work, all of it would be counted mere extravagance, were it not for the extraordinary culinary magic worked in the kitchen by her husband, Arthur, and his magical woks.

When, that is, his amorous temperament didn't get the better of his gonads.

Even now, she could see him at the kitchen door, struggling to move a long table, wok, and sundry arcane accouterments into the main dining room.

"And what the hell are you doing?" she demanded loudly, rounding the smorgasbord with a look that would have straightened the Great Wall without losing a brick.

Artie Chong only smiled.

He was a solidly medium-height man whose luxurious, long thick hair reminded all who met and saw him of a slightly bizarre country-western singer who'd eaten his fringe. His face was hard-life rugged and clean-shaven, his frame lean without sacrificing an impression of so-so strength, and his locally hand-tailored clothes never changed from day to day— ruffled white shirt, snug black pants, black socks and shoes, all superseded and accented by a preacher's black frock coat with velvet lapels. He was, he claimed to anyone who asked, a Chinese missionary to Occidental lousy taste.

"I asked you a question," his wife said sternly, arms folded across her bosom.

"My darling, I am bereft without you," he declared through the smile. "I cannot work back there any longer. I must see you in all your glory."

"Art, you're a jackass."

"I miss you," he beamed.

"You're still a jackass."

He stood behind the table and stir-fried a few vegetables. "But my love, my passion, my dusky bamboo baby, all I want is just a closer wok with thee."

On a much slower night, in the middle of a raging snow-storm in December, Sophia would have melted, would have cast aside her voluminous apron and her molded silk dress, unloosed the ivory pins that held up her hair, and charged him before he'd even readied the chopsticks. Tonight, however, even so close to closing time at eleven, there were over one hundred customers at the Pagoda's troughs, and she had no time for frivolity.

She grabbed the edge of the table and shoved it back toward the kitchen.

Artie grinned and winked at her as the table struck his midsection. "Is this American foreplay?"

She glared. "Back inside, Art! We've people to feed, in case you hadn't noticed."

"I only have eyes for you," he vowed.

Perhaps.

But as she crammed him back where he belonged, she caught a glimpse of the unconscionably svelte Sordette Biletto bending over the fortune cookie oven. Eyes for his wife, hands for whatever else moved on two female legs, she thought sourly, and was instantly ashamed. In all their years of marriage, Arthur had never given her doubts as to his fidelity to their conjugal union, except for the time he fed water chestnuts to the mayor's wife with his toes at the Police and Firemen Annual Softball Picnic, and the time he pinched Chita Juarel thrice on the rump as he reached for the salt and pepper during a lunch break last week, and the time Sordette was found somewhat, but not entirely, naked in the batter vat for mu-shu pork pancakes.

Damn, she thought, and all shame fled: the man was the horniest bastard ever to leave the Chinese mainland, she loved the little lug passionately, and there was nothing she could do about it. It was her fiery Mediterranean nature.

He threw her a kiss.

She caught it in her palm, pressed it to her cheek, and said, "Get to work!" Lovingly.

Artie nodded with a rueful smile and took his place behind a long table strung with cooking implements. "I am sorry, O Lotus of my Life. I have forgotten my place." He struck himself on the forehead. "Dumb, dumb, dumb, dumb. I'll wok the line."

"See that you do," she muttered, glared at Sordette, who was in training as the Pagoda's first female chef, and returned to the main dining room.

She smiled.

Glasses were emptied, plates were cleaned, seconds were ordered, and soon enough the Chongs would have enough money in the bank to build that long-awaited love nest on the eight acres they'd already purchased on the summit of Gander Mountain. Soon. With luck, by the end of summer. And then they would burn to the ground the sod house her father had given them in a fit of Catholic guilt, sow the front yard with salt, and donate the land to the town.

A dream, she thought, devoutly to be desired.

"Sophia!"

She blinked, put on her best professional smile, and made her way to the central section, first booth, and clasped her hands in dutiful respect to the redheaded man and woman, and the redheaded child, seated there.

"Mr. Mayor," she greeted. "I trust you are enjoying our humble fare this evening?"

"As always, superb, simply superb!" pronounced James Ellader, kissing his pudgy pink fingers loudly and blowing the greasy tribute at the rococo ceiling. "A feast truly fit for a king, not a poor mayor."

"Daddy," Janis Ellader whined, "you're not poor! Are you? Are you poor?" She wrinkled her freckled nose. "Are we poor, Mommy?"

Eunice Ellader spoke from the chokehold her foxhead wrap had about her throat: "No, darling, we are not poor."

"But Daddy said we were."

"It was a figure of speech," the mayor explained, patting his daughter on the head.

"And a fine one it was, Your Honor," Sophia said quickly. "I am pleased you are pleased."

"Quite," said the mayor's wife.

"Neat," said Janis, shoving a handful of noodles into her mouth.

Sophia smiled, bowed, backed away, and looked toward the front window just as a monstrous burst of vivid purple light streaked through town, and a fierce explosion soon after plunged the restaurant into instant darkness. Customers wailed their fright, plates fell and shattered, a booth was torn from its mooring on the wall, the ferns popped from their soil, plaster showered onto the tables, the plate-glass window cracked corner to corner, and Sordette screamed from the kitchen, "Holy shit, Art, that was a good one!"

Casopia Gumpers stood beneath a streetlamp on the corner of Main Street and Hickory Lane and checked her face in the mirror of her compact. It wasn't a bad face, even in this light. In fact, it was a face much envied by those ordinary women of Gander Pond, those housewives and secretaries and librarians and clerks who worked dawn to dusk for minimum wage and a prick for a boss. The eyebrows were arched, the blue eyes smoky, the nose aristocratic without being off-putting, the lips scarlet and desirable, the chin just gentle enough to demand a soft squeeze.

And the rest of her wasn't all that bad either.

She knew it.

She had known it since childhood, and since childhood had learned to exploit her subtle attractiveness without the slightest feeling of guilt or remorse. And since it generally worked, she hadn't once entertained doubts that couldn't be dismissed by a perusal of her passbook.

She had graduated in the top fourth of her class in high school, the top fifth in college, and the top seventh in graduate school; her first two husbands had lasted three years each before they wore out; the third one had joined the Canadian Army; the fourth had vanished into the Idaho Rockies and had never been seen again with a human being. "Prowess" was what one of them had told her, reaching for the oxygen tank beside the bed; "You got too much goddamned prowess, woman." Which, when she checked it out, translated into "skill." Which, when she tested it, translated into the penthouse at the Gander Palace, the Silver Cloud in the private garage, and the wall of safety-deposit boxes at Gander Federal on Hemlock Avenue.

The compact disappeared into her purse.

She sighed, rolled her shoulders, and ran a slow hand down the side of her tastefully red dress—a gossamer summer frock with puffed sleeves denoting a hint of innocence, a décolletage modest yet provocative, a snug waist that cried out for holding, and a flared skirt she had trained to swirl and lift just so. It was, she admitted without false modesty, a killer, and one she had made herself from a simple pattern her mother had left her, though truthfully, her mother had counseled zippers in the instructions, not Velcro.

A gentle breeze coyly tousled her hair and sent ripples along her skirt, and she looked east along Main Street, to the bright lights of Restaurant Row, the now dark marquee of the movie theater, the windows of the shops displaying more neon than goods this time of night.

Then she looked west, to the next intersection, where each corner was taken up by a hotel, none more than four stories, none with a single room available to the casual traveler. This, she knew, was the height of Gander Pond's tourist season—the carnival was whooping it up just outside town to the south, the lakes to the north were just warm enough for swimming and filled enough for fishing, the woods were packed with game, the days warm, the nights muggy, the food and drink the best one could have for twenty miles.

A contented sigh as she leaned against the lamppost and brushed a lock of startling blonde hair away from her eyes. Ordinarily she would have made her way either to the Gander Hi-Lite, the Mountain Resort, the Greenland Glen, or the Rest-and-Rec. A seat in one of the lounges, an unlit cigarette, and she would be open for business. But not tonight. Tonight she was slumming, succumbing to what she knew was an irrational desire to see how the other half did it.

It was humiliating.

People *talked* to her.

People *looked* at her.

People for god's sake *asked her for directions*!

A laughing crowd of young adults boiled out of the Taco Supreme and made their way unsteadily along the other side of the street.

Three men in pink bowling shirts rounded the corner, nudged each other when they saw her, and continued west, toward the hotels.

Music from the band at Marcello's, from the jukebox at the Stagger Inn, from radios on shoulders, stereos in automobiles, open-windowed apartments over the shops, hums from passersby; boots and shoes on the pavement, wheels on the blacktop; conversations; dogs yapping and night birds trilling and if it didn't stop soon she would go out of her mind.

I think, she decided, I need a vacation.

"Good evening."

She didn't turn. She had heard the heels approaching as soon as the traffic signal changed.

"I had hoped our talk the other night would have . . . altered your opinion."

She waited.

Eventually a woman moved to stand in front of her—a short woman dressed in black jeans and a blue plaid shirt, thick black shoes, and a contemporary short wimple that made her young face seem more severe than it was.

"Sister," Casopia said, not unkindly, "bug off."

Sister Lillian Vorth lifted an eyebrow and shook her head sadly, though not without a faint smile at her pale lips. "You protest too much, Casopia."

Casopia returned the smile in spite of the dent the nun's appearance would surely put in her affairs. They had first spoken three evenings ago, at the exclusive Chairman Lounge of the Greenland Glen, a favorite meeting place for the town's more prosperous pols and merchants, and those visitors who wanted to buy more than just live bait. Casopia had been working on a dish of unsalted peanuts, a Bloody Mary, and county newspaper magnate Horace O'Malley when Sister Lillian began whispering biblical verses in her ear. O'Malley had finally left. Casopia had had another drink.

"If I were to protest, Sister," she said, "you'd know it."

The nun's smile broadened knowingly. "Ah. I am reaching you, yes?"

"Not hardly."

"But you are thinking, true?"

"Not what you think."

Sister Lillian glanced up and down the street, then at the stars barely visible above them. "I shall, you realize, be your shadow from now on."

"Why?"

"Because," the woman said earnestly, "I see in you a basically kindhearted woman who has, in the rough course of her life, gone astray." The smile turned beatific. "And I have appeared at this fortuitous time to set you back onto the path of awakening."

Casopia tucked her purse under one arm. "Sister, the only

awakening I'm going to get is a rude one if I can't meet my margin call on Monday.''

''Your stock always rises with me,'' the nun told her.

''Bull,'' Casopia said cheerfully, and eased around her to head for the vaguely tree-shaped Mountain Resort. Single tourists congregated there, bored to death of fishing, too scared to go camping, and wishing to hell they'd stayed in Philadelphia where at least bored-to-hell was status quo. She therefore appeared like unto Los Angeles to them.

''Casopia, don't do this thing.''

She walked on, adjusting her hip-swing, her arm-swing, her torso-swing. By the time she reached the hotel's bar, she'd be wound up and ready.

''Casopia, I beg of you!''

She fluffed her hair and tilted her head so it would catch the light from the barber pole as she passed it.

''Casopia, you will be *punished*!''

Good lord, I hope not, she thought as she waited at the next corner for the light to change; all I want to do is lie down.

The traffic signal changed—from red to purple.

The concussion aftermath of a distant huge explosion knocked her to her knees.

''Jesus,'' she gasped.

And Sister Lillian laughed maniacally as all the lights went out.

At the ranch house rectory and part-time halfway house of the Holy Spirit Today Tabernacle Society, the Reverends Phil and Phyllis Lager sat on their wicker bench swing on their back porch and watched the sky over Gander Mountain explode in glorious purple exaltation.

''Well, well, well,'' said Phil as a fierce wind blew in the windows behind them and plastered him to the swing, ''it seems we called it after all.''

His wife, pleated skirt blown up around her waist and cheeks flubbering, disagreed. ''It's four years late.''

''But to the day, darling.''

''Four years.''

''To the day.''

''Four.''

"The flock won't care. The Judgment is clearly upon us, and we made the prophecy."

"The flock," she groused, "is a muscle-bound cop, a wino, four pairs of identical twins, and fifty-six old farts who drool on the hymnals."

"They will be pleased."

"They will be dead."

Phil considered for a moment, stroking his long brown beard, then his long brown hair. "I suppose." He looked to his wife. "But if they're not . . ."

Phyllis considered for a moment.

Then she grinned.

When darkness lay complete upon the heavily wooded slopes of Gander Mountain, there wasn't a hell of a lot to see. It was a natural phenomenon Benny Hart hadn't counted on when he climbed the not quite steep north side earlier that afternoon. He also hadn't counted on getting hopelessly lost. After all, he thought as he blundered into his fifth or sixth birch in the past five or six minutes, this ain't the Rockies, for Christ's sake. I'm not trying to get to the top of Mount lousy Everest, for crying out loud.

He tripped over a rock and fell, momentarily pinned to the ground by a backpack he'd liberated from its political cell in Melmortski's Hardware and Camping Supplies. When he finally rolled over, he stared at what he could see of the sky through the black foliage and decided to call it a day. The ground here was reasonably flat, he was reasonably exhausted, and there was no telling what he'd find when he reached Krutch Hollow.

With luck, not MaryLou Krutch.

If she was there, he was a dead man.

But if she was on her vacation the way she was supposed to be, he was a rich man. A very rich man. Not only the richest man in Gander Pond, but quite possibly the richest man on the Eastern Seaboard. The notion made him tremble. He closed his eyes and took several deep breaths in order to calm himself.

Rich.

No more sneaking around at night, breaking into innocent people's houses, stealing their life's savings, shattering their

dreams, denying their children a college education; no more
traveling to New York in order to pawn the jewelry and tro-
phies he'd liberated from their middle-class dungeons; no
more ink stains from those horrid fingerprinting sessions.
God, he hated getting his hands dirty!

Rich.

And all because MaryLou Krutch was not only a miser by
repute, she was a tightwad in fact. And after twenty years
living alone on the mountain with minimal contact with the
outside world, there was no question that she'd amassed a
horde of wealth crying out to be freed from the bondage of
nonspending. The thought of it made his teeth ache. Here she
was, a woman, a sort of free-form capitalist, who denied the
economy's wheels of commerce their much-needed grease,
thus throwing God alone knew how many impoverished men
out of work, causing untold deprivation and anguish among
women and children of either sex, and plunging entire com-
munities into a depression which would take generations to
dissipate.

It was, then, his goddamn Republican duty to steal. From
her. As long as she wasn't home to blow his head off.

He sat up, dusted himself off, and pulled a flashlight from
a holster at his belt.

He nodded.

The clearing was large enough to hold him, small enough
to hide him, and there were, as far as he could tell, no signs
of hostile bears. If the mosquitoes didn't eat him alive, he
ought to get a good night's sleep. Then onward to the Hollow,
a quick case of the immediate area, and—

He sighed.

He switched off the light.

He switched it on again and said, "Hi."

MaryLou Krutch stepped away from the tree she'd been
leaning against. In her left hand was a Bowie knife, in her
right a shotgun; across her shoulder was slung a crossbow;
around her waist was a utility belt that held a long-bladed
knife, a cosh, two leather pouches, and a grenade. She wore
a black T-shirt, black denims, black boots, and a black beret
with a pheasant feather poked through the center.

"You lost?" she said.

He nodded weakly.

"You looking for me?"

He shook his head.

"You lying?"

He nodded.

"You a stud?"

He blinked.

"Don't move."

He didn't.

She knelt in front of him, placing the rifle on the ground, just out of his reach. A thoughtful grunt, and she pulled out her own flashlight and ran its beam over him from head to toe and back again, nodding all the while. Then she pointed the Bowie knife at him and said, "Take off your pack."

There was no question of protest; he had been caught in the act, and only her misapprehension that he was some sort of lunatic midnight Lothario prevented him from tearfully confessing the truth of his nocturnal mission. So he swung the pack off his shoulders and handed it over.

"Thanks."

He could say nothing.

"You like the woods?"

He managed a shaky nod.

"I do too."

Another nod.

She sniffed. "Peaceful, you know what I mean? No damned people. Just me and the squirrels."

Right, he thought, and drew his knees casually to his chest, hiding the section of his own belt to which had been clipped a rather unpleasant-looking hammer.

Though she rummaged through his gear with a studied careless air, he knew that she was watching him from the corner of her eye. Any sudden move now would mean his death, or a severe maiming, or at the very least, a good clop to the chops with that wilderness-hardened hand of hers.

And lord, what a hand! Slender but powerful, delicate but with a purpose. Just as the rest of her was, he noted belatedly and with a modicum of astonishment; no Ma Kettle here, no applicant for the AKC. She wasn't beautiful by any means, but even in the harsh glow of the flashlight she was most definitely attractive, for a woman who spent her life trapping and hunting through the remote New Jersey wilds.

She closed the pack and sat down in front of him. "So," she said, "you were gonna rob me, huh?"

"Good grief, no!" he said.

"Sure you were."

"How can you say that? You don't even know me."

She smiled. "Benjamin Hart, right?"

His mouth opened and closed.

"Don't look so surprised. I seen you around. Saw your picture in the papers, last time you was caught." She chuckled. "Pretty damn something or other, trying to rob Artie Chong with his wife still there."

"I was not stealing," he said.

"Paper said you was."

"The paper," he said disdainfully, "is run by an alcoholic lackey of an imperialist local government. He wouldn't know a liberation army if he fell over it. Or into it."

MaryLou nodded sagely. "And I take it you're the liberation army?"

"As best I can be," he admitted with pride.

"Good for you."

"Huh?"

MaryLou squirmed closer until their knees were touching. "I said, good for you." She thrust out her hand. "Nice to meet an army. Especially one what's out to rob from the rich and give to the proletariat."

He searched her eyes for signs of mockery, checked the other hand to make sure it wasn't about to part his ribs with the knife, then took her hand and shook it.

She laughed.

He smiled.

She said, "So. You came all the way up here to liberate my treasure, huh?"

In truth, he could no longer deny it. This woman was clearly far too clever in the wiles of the wild. Better he should be honest.

"Yes," he said.

She boxed his ears.

When he was finally able to leap-stagger to his feet, ready to take her on even if she was a woman, she had already picked up the rifle and aimed it at the middle of his wavering forehead.

"Hold still," she ordered.

"Doing the best I can."

"Not that it makes a difference," she went on. "Blow your head off, blow your face off, makes no nevermind to me one way or the other."

"Well, it makes a hell of a big difference to me," he snapped.

"Benny," she said, "shut up and die right."

"In your hat," he sneered.

And the world suddenly went purple, the mountain bucked and threw him to the ground, and MaryLou Krutch shrieked in terror and threw herself upon him.

"Lord!" she said. "God, you didn't tell me you was a real *army*!"

IT groaned.

IT blacked out.

IT awoke to the sound of metal creaking and cooling, trees falling, birds screaming, animals running, fire snapping and snarling both inside and out.

IT dragged ITself from the wreckage of ITs craft and waited for ITs vision to clear.

And when it had, IT knew that IT had reached ITs destination.

It knew that soon, very soon, the killing would begin.

" 'Ey, Pancho," IT said to ITself in clear delight, in a voice unheard since Edison could hear, "go saddle the horses. We ride at dawn."

ꞏ2ꞏ

"God, I'm dying!" was less an exclamation of dismay than it was a complaint.

"You're not dying."

He groaned as something jabbed a needle into his skull. "I am dying, god, I'm dying."

"Nope."

He kept his eyes tightly closed, though the sparks there burned him. "I am dying," he said carefully, "and I shall not see Scotland again."

"Trust me. I know these things, I used to work in a bar. You are not dying."

"Bloody hell!" He sat up, glowered, winced, and grabbed the back of his head to keep it from falling off. With his other hand he grabbed his forehead to keep *it* from falling off. Then he searched for a third hand to smack the blurred face of the woman kneeling beside him. "God, how the hell can you call this not dying?"

"For crying out loud, Kent," she said in disgust, "the Russians have dropped The Bomb and all you can do is lie there and think of dying."

Footsteps stomped angrily across the terrace. He heard the woman yelp, heard echoes of an explosion, and cautiously opened one eye in hopes of finding a pile of cinders in her place. When there wasn't, he decided he wasn't dying, he was already dead, in Hell, with his favorite bathrobe reduced to little more than a lapel and a belted loincloth.

"Goddamn Russians," Chita said, slumping against the railing.

"Bombs," he told her patiently, "are not purple."

Nevertheless, he was forced to admit that something damned near like a bomb had struck nearby. The terrace was littered with broken glass, broken wind chimes, wood chips, leaves, clots of dirt, and the unmistakable black fur of an unmasked raccoon. As he pushed himself unsteadily to his feet, he also noticed that the railing was slightly bent. Inward.

"Are you all right?" he asked, belting what remained of his singed robe about his waist.

"Just stepped on something, that's all," she muttered. "I'll live. I think." She wasn't naked anymore. She wore a baggy white shirt, and jeans that weren't baggy by any stretch of the imagination.

"You should wear shoes," he said as he looked over the parking lot to Gander Mountain.

"I didn't exactly have time," she said. "There was a bomb, remember?"

The sky above the mountain glowed. Pulsed. Vibrated. In purple.

Yet there didn't seem to be any fire.

"You know," he said thoughtfully, "I don't think that was a bomb."

"Oh sure," Chita said, hauling herself to her feet. "It was a shooting star, right?"

He pointed. "That plane, remember? It had purple lights."

"Which one?"

"The one over the mountain."

"There?" She pointed at the sky.

"No," he snapped, and pointed at the mountain. "There."

"Oh. Hey, it's purple!"

"The plane was purple."

She frowned. "So where's the plane?"

"There," he told her, and grabbed her arm before she could point again. "I think it's crashed. In fact, I'm sure of it."

"So," she said, "what kind of a plane crashes purple?"

It was an enigma, and one he was sure the local authorities could deal with quite well. For his own part, his head ached, his back ached, and the eerie glow above the trees was giving him eyestrain. No doubt there would be something on the radio or television to explain it. In the more immediate meantime, there was this horrid mess to clean up, clothes to put on, and medication to take if he was to function well enough to get some sleep tonight.

Sirens wailed in the distance.

He listened for a moment, turned around, and did his best not to scream—the glass doors had been blown inward, the chantilly drapes shredded, and he could see the insides of his couch spilling bloblike onto the carpet. He clasped his hands. He raised his chin. He walked slowly inside where, avoiding the debris he supposed he ought to be glad he could barely see, he tried to switch on the jade double-elephant lamp, the ivory tiger lamp, the freestanding chrome lamp, and the ceiling light in the kitchen. To his dismay, none of them worked. Then he tried the radio, the television, the telephone, the vent in the bathroom, and, back in the living room, the electric player piano, again without significant success.

"Well, blast!"

His first thought was that he'd forgotten to pay the damned bill again; his second, that whatever had perhaps crashed on the mountain's summit must have knocked down a hell of a lot of power lines; his third, that Chita was standing awfully close behind him.

He turned.

She smiled at him toothsomely, and he was amazed at how accurately her complexion reflected the sky's bizarre glow.

"So," she wanted to know, "we going out there to see what's going on, or do you want to party?"

"That," he said coldly, "is rather a hedonistic way of facing possible disaster, wouldn't you say?"

"You think we're going to die?"

She didn't seem very concerned, and to avoid that smile, those teeth, those lips, he glanced over her head to the mountain. "To be honest . . . no."

More sirens, and the sound of a helicopter flying rapidly overhead.

"On the other hand, we might be able to help."

"Oh." She placed a hand on one of his lapels. "You a doctor or something?"

"No, just a simple humanitarian."

The other hand slithered to the other lapel. "You know, I did come all the way up here to see if you were all right. I did do that, you know."

Not wanting to seem ungrateful, he gave her a swift but enchanting smile. "Indeed you did, and I am truly touched." Then he gently took her wrists and lowered her arms to her sides. "It was quite selfless of you."

"I know. So what are you going to do about it?"

It was then that he realized that a decision had to be made. On the one hand, his efforts to date Chita seemed finally to have achieved some sort of fruition, though this was hardly the ideal situation—unless one was crass enough to consider standing clothed in only a tattered bathrobe in front of a lovely woman an ideal situation; on the other hand, the longer he stared at the mountain's purple majesty, the more curious he became about its origin, its implication.

This could be the chance of a lifetime, something he ought not to miss, something he might be able to tell his grand-children, if his mother let him live that long.

Still, Chita was hardly chopped liver.

Yet, extraordinary explosions of purple didn't happen every night.

He looked down; he looked up; he looked down; he looked up; Chita grabbed his belt and yanked until his chin rested against her forehead.

"Now listen," she said huskily into his throat—and a damned erotic feeling that was, he was bound to admit—"if you don't plan on doing anything to me right at the moment, the least you can do is offer me a ride out there in that ugly car of yours."

"It is not ugly," he insisted to her hair.

"It has reindeer horns on the roof."

Gently he pushed her away; silently he signaled her to wait while he dressed; frantically, and in the dark, he dressed in a white shirt and jeans, realized that he looked like her, changed the shirt to a dark brown one, yanked on hand-tooled tan western boots, grabbed a denim jacket from the closet, and bumped into Chita in the hallway.

"What now?" he demanded.

"Thought you might need help. You took so long."

"I am fine, thank you very much." He brushed past her, reached back for her hand, and led her to the door. "Tell me something, are you always this forward?"

"Me? I'm not forward."

"You were trying to spy on me in the privacy of my boudoir."

She shrugged, very slowly. "I just wanted to know what a lord's bed looked like."

He willed himself not to plant a fist atop her head. "If you must know, I am not a lord. I am a baron."

"Honey," she said, opening the door and shoving him out, "you can be a king for all I care. You still don't got nothing I ain't seen already."

He closed the door, made sure it was locked. "I wouldn't be too sure about that." And decided that a gentleman would ignore the knowing grunt that followed, blaming it instead on the clouds of choking dust that swirled through the hallway.

Because of the electrical failure, the elevators weren't working, so they chose the fire stairs, stopping at her floor so she could get a pair of tennis shoes before continuing on. Their footsteps echoed. The air here was no less clogged, no more breathable. And they met no one along the way, which he thought was passing strange; surely someone would have panicked and tried to flee, or find help.

And the ornate, brass and marble lobby with its fifteen-foot laminated monochrome photograph of the young King Tut on the wall was equally deserted.

"Curious," he said, pausing to look around. "I wonder why no one else is here."

"No one else wants to get blown up," she told him sourly.

"We will not be blown up, my dear. The explosion has already occurred."

He nodded to the glittering islands of glass on the floor, the gouges in the marble-veneer walls, and to the gaps where the floor-to-ceiling windows had once been, the holes where the revolving doors used to be, and the space on the left where the security guard's smoked-glass desk once stood.

The guard was gone as well.

"The guard is gone," Chita noted as they stepped gingerly over the debris. "You think he knows something?"

The glow had diminished considerably; the night was almost dark again.

"I don't know." A guiding gesture, and they made for the parking lot's far, unlighted corner. "Perhaps he was injured."

"I didn't see no blood."

"Then perhaps he's all right."

"So why isn't he guarding us against looters? And," she added a minute later, "they are so reindeer horns."

He refused to argue, only waved her brusquely into the car, and for luck patted the impressive rack of antlers welded to the roof. It wasn't his fault that the dealer he purchased the vehicle from had had so little to offer in his price range; and it wasn't his fault that the previous owner of this four-door sedan liked neon red; and it most assuredly was not his personal choice to have the seats covered in tie-dyed sheepskin. Ordinarily he would have chosen a sedate Jaguar sedan, no horns, and genuine leather. As it was, he had this, and over the years he'd grown quite fond of it, and protective of it, and felt no qualms at all at naming it Dilemma.

It started immediately.

"Jesus, this stuff itches," Chita complained.

"You want to walk?"

"You got gas?"

"Only here," he muttered, thumping a fist against his chest.

She slouched with a grunt, folded her arms across her breasts, and glared out the windshield as he sped skillfully from the lot, turned toward the newly paved highway that led through Gander Pass, and switched on the radio in hopes of finding some information.

There was nothing but static.

Chita straightened.

Kent noticed there were no other cars on the road, only a scattering of fallen branches, fallen twigs.

Chita leaned forward and looked at the sky.

Kent stomped on the brakes, and she slammed into the glass, bounced back, and slugged his arm.

"Jesus, you nearly killed me!"

"Chita—"

She slugged his arm again. "I'm gonna have a bruise, for god's sake! You know what kind of tips a bruise gets?"

"Chita—"

"And who the hell are those guys?"

He wasn't sure.

He only knew that the place where the road swung sharply to the right and began its steep climb up the mountain was one hundred yards ahead. But fifty yards ahead an intricate arrangement of orange-striped sawhorses had been stretched across the blacktop. And behind it stood more than a dozen men in uniform, three idling Jeeps, and what he could only describe as a bloody big tank.

All of the men had rifles.

All the rifles were aimed at his car.

Meticulously, as the voice of the forest slowly returned to normal, IT surveyed ITs craft in the light IT would never know was purple. Slowly IT walked around it and the crater it had made, ignoring the licking flames, the suffocating smoke. This, IT knew, was going to be a problem.

But IT had faced problems before, and IT had always conquered them.

IT was not afraid.

Then part of the engine blew up, and IT said to ITself, "Beev, we're in trouble."

"Are you all right?"

At first Casopia thought she had finally made direct contact with the Other Side—a kind voice, a tender tone; it almost sounded sweet. Then, when the question was repeated, she sensed someone kneeling beside her and thought that asking about one's health when one had just been blown off the face of the Earth was in rather poor taste.

"Excuse me? Are you hurt?"

A tentative hand touched her shoulder.

The street scraped her cheek and she winced.

Angels, she thought, are flying too damned close to the ground.

Abruptly she grinned—well, hot damn, she wasn't dead after all. To be sure, her cheek and palms burned, her ears rang, there were flares of purple behind her eyes, and she was positive her careful coif had been permanently rearranged; but at least she wasn't dead.

"Miss?"

She stirred.

"Are you all right? Should I get a doctor? I am a doctor, actually, but I'm not a doctor. Should I get one?"

And since she was, in fact, still alive, she supposed she ought to be grateful that the concerned citizen wasn't Sister Lillian; it was a man. With a groan then that required no acting, she pushed herself to her hands and knees, assisted by strong fingers at her waist. She waited, didn't throw up, and allowed the Samaritan to guide her to her feet.

"Jesus," she said.

"Exactly!" screamed Sister Lillian behind her.

Casopia's vision cleared almost instantly, and her breath was short-circuited by two immediate stunning visions: the first was Main Street, a horrifying vista reminiscent of unchecked calamity, complete with ominously darkened storefronts, torn papers blown by the wind, broken glass in the gutters, dismembered mannequins, and not a few revelers scattered and moaning all over the blacktop; the second was the gentleman gazing concernedly into her eyes. If beautiful could be applied to men, she thought, this guy was it. From his somewhat artfully disheveled blond hair to his deep mountain tan, he was absolutely gorgeous in a nonrugged sort of way; from his pale yellow shirt, white pants, white shoes, and lavender sport jacket with sleeves rolled to the elbow and bulging pockets, however, he was a disaster, if not a real estate agent.

"Hooker," he said shyly.

"Hey," she snapped. "Jeez, I just got killed almost. Give a lady a break."

Shyness switched to genuine consternation. "Oh heavens, no, miss. I didn't mean . . . not you, really . . . that is, *I'm* Hooker. Nicodemus Hooker." He gestured vaguely behind him. "I was on my way back to my room from the taco place when the . . . whatever happened."

"Punishment," the nun shrieked.

Casopia looked to the corner and saw Sister Lillian fervently embracing the lamppost. Her wimple was askew, her jeans gaped at the knees, and her eyes were startlingly wide.

"That often happens," Hooker said beside her, "when the world ends."

"The world's ended?" Casopia stared at him in alarm.

The man's expression was apologetic. "I'm sorry, forgive me, it was a jest. I couldn't help it. People often do that too, in the face of the inexplicable and unthinkable. They do it in the movies all the time."

Sirens filled the night.

Patrons stumbled out of the restaurants, bars, lounges, alleys.

The weird purple and pulsing glow in the sky began to fade, but not fast enough for Casopia's taste. Without thinking, she took the man's arm in both hands and held on. She was trembling, and there was a distinct feel of autumn in the air. Part of it, she knew, was due to the fact that her puffed sleeves had been reduced to little more than ankle straps, and that her flared skirt had been slit rather daringly up both sides, nearly to her hips.

It was the other part she didn't want to think about.

"So what was it?"

"A crash of some kind," Hooker theorized. "I was in the midst of a lifelong dream when quite without warning something large and purple flashed overhead. I couldn't tell what it was. A second later came the light and the explosion." He frowned thoughtfully. "I am sorely tempted to go up there and find out what happened."

"Oh no you don't, pal," she protested quickly, hugging his arm more tightly. "You're not leaving me now that you've saved me."

Hooker seemed confused. "Did I save you?"

"Lord, where is Thy raiment!"

"Damn right," she said. "And now I owe you a drink."

Sheepishly the man confessed that he did not imbibe, the better to preserve his lifelong dream.

Incredulously she asked if he was some sort of religious fanatic.

"Oh no, not really. Perhaps only in the secular sense."

"Never heard of them."

"I'm a scientist."

"Them I've heard of. And most of them drink like fish."

Hooker shrugged. "A failing, I admit. I just never learned to acquire the taste."

A pair of fire engines swung into view at the far end of the street, a yellow '34 Cord squealed around a corner and nearly took out a fire hydrant, and a police cruiser whipped past with all lights flashing.

The purple glow faded even more.

Suddenly Casopia felt her legs give way, but before she reached the ground, Hooker swept her up in his arms and cradled her close to his chest. She placed a grateful head on his shoulder. He stared at the chaos for several seconds more before carrying her to the pavement, where, instead of putting her down, he adjusted his hold and muttered to himself.

Sister Lillian sagged to the pavement, tears streaming down her begrimed face. "Lord!" she bellowed.

Casopia closed her eyes. It was comforting, actually, listening to all those trigonometric formulae pass his lips in a litany of scientific speculation. She hadn't heard anything like that since the afternoon of her quantum physics final, when her professor suggested that practical application rather than theory was the best way to discover what she had learned.

She already knew.

He had learned a few tricks himself.

"You know," she said dreamily, "I don't know what that lifelong dream of yours is, but do you think we could discuss it over dinner?"

Hooker pointed with his chin. "Even if I were so inclined after such an event, miss, you'll note that there is no viable electricity left in town."

"There's more than one way to light a fire."

She sensed his gaze then, sensed his desire, sensed that neither of them had anything to do with her. She debated. She felt his heartbeat. She snuggled, and, understanding quite well that she was about to make a damned fool of herself, she whispered, "Then how about we go up there and find out what's going on?"

"You mean it?"

She smiled. "Of course. Only a dope would pass up an opportunity like this."

Gently he placed her on her feet. "Casopia, would you really do that for me?"

"What the hell," she said.

He took her shoulders.

She felt her legs threaten to give again. "I have a car."

"So do I. Mind if I drive?"

Sister Vorth staggered past them, coughed, and paused to say, "I knew I should have been an Episcopalian," before disappearing around the corner.

This is dumb, girl, Casopia warned, yet did not hesitate to follow Hooker to the garage of the Greenland, to a two-seater red convertible sports car which he wheeled expertly into the debris-strewn street.

He drove cautiously.

A fire engine company battled a second-story blaze in a hardware store; an ambulance had parked askew at the curb in front of the twenty-four-hour delicatessen, and the attendants were lifting a stretcher into the back; from the hotels and restaurants, patrons wandered into the streets, their voices raised in fearful babble; a police car had positioned itself in the center of Gander's main intersection, and a patrolman, his face pale but determined, used the car's radio to report on the scene before him.

Casopia saw Sophia Chong climb gingerly through the ruins of the Pagoda's front window, her hair unbunned and caught in the wind; she saw Horace O'Malley throw a trash can through the newspaper's front door and clamber through; she blew a kiss at the cop; she blew a kiss at O'Malley's back; she blew a kiss at Nick, whose gaze never wavered from the purple glow in the sky.

Once they were out of town, however, the scientist's caution was swiftly abandoned. Gears slipped through their paces, the engine shifted from a purr to a roar, and soon the wind whipped her hair, caressed her cheeks, brought with it the distinct odor of burning wood and scorched metal.

"What do you think it is?" she yelled over the noise of car and wind.

He took a moment to answer. "I'm not sure."

"Man," she said with a shake of her head, "that's out of this world, y'know?"

Suddenly his right hand grabbed her knee tightly. So tightly she gasped.

"What do you mean by that?" he demanded.

"Nothing," she answered. "Nick, watch the road."

"You must have meant something." Beauty had become the beast. He wasn't pretty when he was angry.

She tried to move his hand; it clamped harder.

"Damnit, Nick, it's just an expression, for Christ's sake!"

He stared.

She pointed at the turn fast approaching.

His eyes narrowed in thought.

She grabbed his chin and swiveled his head around to the front.

The sleek automobile took the turn easily, smoothly, though she noted that they had come awfully close to swiping the rear fender off a police cruiser nose-down in a shallow ditch.

"I'm sorry," he apologized, releasing his tension with a visible effort. "Truly, I am sorry."

"No sweat," she said. "But god, I don't get it."

"It's my dream."

"Ah." She nodded without understanding a thing. "Ah."

"Aliens."

"In New Jersey?" She frowned. "Well, I suppose in the cities, but I thought there was a law—"

"No," he said, sweeping through an S-curve barely wide enough for hope. He pointed to the stars. "Aliens."

Oh shit, she thought; oh nuts.

A fallen tree forced them to slow, to maneuver around the exposed roots, half of which were afire.

"I am not crazy," he said once they'd regained speed.

Her answering smile was tolerably real.

"I don't believe in them," he went on.

Now she was perplexed.

"I just want to meet one."

Now she was confused, but she said nothing. The road had become as a pretzel, and she had no intention of capturing any of his concentration while he made his way closer to the crash site. On the other hand, she had seen many things in her short lifetime, experienced many of life's exhilarating as well as seedy aspects, but nothing had prepared her for the way his right hand worked the gearshift so expertly.

"God, you're good," she said breathlessly.

"I've been driving for years," he explained proudly.

"Looking for aliens," she said flatly.

"Later," he told her. "I will explain all later."

Ten minutes after his enigmatic promise, they pulled up behind another red car—with horns on its roof—which in turn had been stopped by an awesome roadblock manned by over a dozen soldiers.

"Aha," Hooker said quietly.

Then one of the soldiers aimed a rifle at his head.

On the sidewalk, Sophia stood helplessly amid the wreckage of her window. Her arms flapped uselessly. Her lips quivered. She wept. She wept for the desolation she saw along Main Street, for the injured and the lost, and for the dent in their savings the repairs were going to hammer. Now they would never get out of that damned sod house, and this she couldn't even blame on Art and his spendthrift ways.

She whirled, suddenly afraid.

"Art!"

Inside, through billowing clouds of dust and smoke, she could see her customers helping each other up, brushing away plaster and glass and bits of shredded plant life. None seemed seriously injured.

"Art!"

Ellader and his family hurried through the nonexistent door, the mayor telling his wife to take the child home, he had a town to save and the newspeople to see.

"What newspeople, Daddy?" little Janis asked, wide-eyed.

"The newspeople who will put Daddy on television for the next hundred years, if I have anything to say about it," he told her tenderly. Then he rushed off, screaming at storeowners to stop cleaning up until the cameras arrived.

Mrs. Ellader looked at Sophia and said proudly, "He's a prick, I'll grant you, but he's my man," and hustled her daughter away.

"Art, damnit!"

And he was there, his black outfit unscathed, his face twisted with distress until he saw her. He ran through the window and leapt into her arms. He felt good. She felt him again, and he still felt good.

"Oh, Art," she whispered.

"Not to worry, O Rose of my Chestnut Garden, not to worry."

"But all this—"

"Will be cleaned in a jiffy, my darling. We will pull together. We will make things right." He looked to the sky. "So what happened?"

She turned in the comfort of his arm, and they looked eastward, toward the mountain. "I don't know. It looks like something crashed up there."

"It's purple," he said in amazement.

She shrugged.

His voice deepened. "Perhaps someone is hurt."

She stiffened.

"Perhaps, while you attend to the Pagoda, I will—"

"Stay right here," she ordered. "Art, this is none of your business."

He stepped away and put his hands on her shoulders. "I am part owner, yes?"

"That's not what I meant."

"And as part owner," he continued, unruffled, "it is part of my part owner's duty to assess any situation that may add to my profits, yes?"

Sophia squirmed. "Well, I guess, but what does that—"

He pointed. "If there are rescuers up there, my Blossom of the Garden State, they will need sustenance, yes?" And he smiled wisely.

She returned the smile with a chuckle. "Art. You little devil, you."

He tapped his temple. "I do not always think, but when I do think, I *think*." He glanced at the street. "I think I don't know how to get there."

Sophia remembered the tramp Gumpers freewheeling it out of town just a few minutes ago with some guy she had never seen before; she recalled a police cruiser wailing toward Gander Mountain not five minutes earlier; she remembered the car keys in her purse, and Art's inability to drive for more than a hundred yards without stripping the gears and any passengers he might be carrying.

"Walk," she suggested.

"At a time like this?" He threw his arms wide. "My darling, my life, my sweet-and-sour Sophia, how can you think of cooking when all about us is collapsing?"

"You brought it up," she reminded him.

"I did. But not now."

"Walk," she repeated.

He started for the kitchen.

With a groan, she grabbed his shoulders, spun him around, and aimed him up the street. And pushed whilst waving a tearful goodbye.

"Ah!" he exclaimed. He looked over his shoulder. "You Americans are terribly clever, you know."

She shooed him.

"But how," he called, "am I to get back once I have seen what we will need?"

"You'll find a way," she answered. "Just think about the house."

"Sod it," he muttered.

"Not in my lifetime," she declared grimly, and returned inside to find a broom, Sordette, and any able-bodied man willing to aid in the restoration of business and community. None denied her.

And the cleanup of Gander Pond began as the sky pulsed purple, and there was thunder in the hills.

"Phil," said the Reverend Phyllis Lager as she picked herself off the porch floor and straightened her pleated skirt, "I've had a revelation."

"Too late," the minister said. His beard was tangled. His long hair was a mess. There were bruises on his chest and legs, and his arms were stiff.

"What," she said, "if that is truly a message from the Lord?"

Phil considered it.

"What," she said, "if it's a flying saucer?"

Phil debated it.

"What," she concluded, "if we were the first ones in the universe to convert a man from Mars?"

He nodded thoughtfully.

"Phil?"

"Could happen," he admitted.

She smiled. "I knew it!"

"Quite a hike, though."

"We'll take the Tabernacle limo."

He doubted.

"Who's going to see?"

He wrestled.

"Besides, it's two miles uphill through the woods, at night, only six on the road in the limo, if I remember my Girl Scouting correctly. We've no time to waste."

"Suppose," he said as he stood, "there aren't any little green men from Mars."

Phyllis shook her head in loving despair. "Phil, you have no faith." She joined him on the top step. "Think about the new church we could build with all the donations. Think about the people we could help. Think about the Lord's will. Think about the poverty-stricken and destitute, the rich and the famous, who will come to us for guidance." She nudged him with an elbow. "Think about it."

For several minutes he did think about it.

"All right," he said at last. "But I get to deliver the sermon."

Phyllis stared at the mountain, stared at her husband, stared at the mountain again and said, "All right. God's will be done."

"Damn right," he said.

IT froze.

Out there in the alien dark, something was moving toward IT.

IT growled deep in ITs throat.

IT had come too far to be thwarted now.

With a disgusted look at ITs crashed craft, and the bits and pieces IT had salvaged in preparation for a miraculous repair job, IT turned to face the forest.

IT sensed that IT was about to be attacked. And though this was not ITs planned battleground, it didn't matter. If the puny inhabitants of the third planet from the star that had caused IT to crash in the first place wanted to take IT on before they even knew what IT was, IT would accommodate them.

After all, that was ITs job.

Death.

Doom.

And total destruction.

"Chester," IT said solemnly, "it's time to clean up this here town."

"Oh . . . god."
John had no idea where he was.
"Oh . . . lord."
One moment he was salivating over his sandwich and praying for dessert, the next he had been blinded by some strange unearthly light that had caused the astonished Officer Twiller to run off the road.

After that . . . nothing.

Now, some time later and he had no idea how long, he was lying on the ground, it was darker than his future, and he could hear the cop somewhere to his left, groaning softly.

The rest, he realized, was silence.

A silence that had him shaking uncontrollably, until he managed to get hold and take a deep breath. Okay, John, he told himself, get it together, man. Be a Smith. Take it slow. One step at a time. At least you're alive. That ought to count for something.

Another deep breath, and the trembling finally ceased.

Twiller groaned, much fainter this time.

With as much delicacy as he could muster, John tested each of his limbs for damage, hissing when his left ankle protested movement. Not broken, he assessed; lightly sprained is all. His head seemed all right. His shoulders felt bruised. There was moisture on his cheek, but he refused to consider the possibility of blood. All in all, he was indeed alive, and for the first time in years, he was glad of it.

He sat up.

He waited for his slightly blurred vision to adjust to the dim purple light.

Oh god, he thought in terror—the woods.

He was back in the woods.

A broad channel of fear opened instantly along his spine, and he looked wildly about him for signs of encroaching ravenous animals bent on savaging his body and dragging him to their lairs. But there was nothing. Not even the night's birds rustled in the leaves.

Calm, he ordered; calm.

Stiffly he struggled to his feet, tested the ankle, and found that it wasn't quite so bad after all. He could hobble without too much pain. Now if he only knew where the damned road was.

A quivering hand rubbed his face.

It was evident that he and Twiller had been more than simply thrown from the cruiser. Somehow, they must have extricated themselves from the wreckage and, most likely dazed and in shock, stumbled into the forest in a blind panic. He recalled nothing of it.

Twiller groaned.

"Lucian!" he called.

A branch fell with a clatter from a tree.

He spun, ignoring the pain.

"Lucian?"

Something moved through the underbrush.

He took a nervous step away from the sound. But it was all around him. Surrounding him. Smothering him. Monsters and bears and bobcats and god knew what else, slowly closing in on him, fangs bared, claws extended, red eyes gleaming in the unmerciful dark.

Suddenly he was desperate for a drink.

"Lucian, you bastard, where the hell are you?"

Lucian groaned, so softly that John wasn't sure he'd really heard it.

The purple light pulsed.

Twiller groaned no more.

A twig snapped then, and so did John.

He ran.

As fast as his injured ankle would permit, he lunged deeper into the forest, panicked and sobbing, colliding with trees, tripping over roots, thrashing through brush that tore at his ragged clothes, not realizing his direction until he saw that the purple glow had grown stronger.

And something terribly large was moving his way.

· 3 ·

"Well, lookie here, Porter," said an earnest young man in knife-crease camouflage fatigues to the taller, stockier, much higher ranked man standing beside him. "Seems we got ourselves some looters."

With a grunt of benign disgust, Master Sergeant Wagoneer slapped the younger man's rifle away. "Ham, you ain't got the brains God gave a clam, you know that?"

He ordered the two dozen men behind him to stand down without relaxing their vigilance.

"But Sarge!" Private First Class Delphim protested.

"Ham," he said with a tight smile, "just watch them, okay? Just watch them, and let me do the talking."

"But Sarge, they could be looters!"

Wagoneer sighed loudly for the amused benefit of the other, more experienced men in his command, then pointed at the dark trees flanking the road. "Now what the hell are they gonna loot, Ham? Acorns?" He glared the green but spunky private out of another response, adjusted his belt, and walked toward one palomino and a line of cars whose headlights did their best to make him squint and lose his night vision. But he would have none of it. He was well versed in such subversive tactics and had trained himself not to react in the expected way.

He was, after all, a professional. A career man. And proud of it.

Slowly, deliberately, aware of curious eyes watching his

every move, he made an elaborate show of unholstering his regulation .45 and holding it loosely at his side. Yet for all his studied nonchalance, every muscle was at the ready, every sense attuned to pick up emanations of possible danger. One never knew what was going to happen, especially when the sky blew up purple. But he was ready. Damnit, he was ready to defend all that was near and dear to him, even if it took every square inch of Ham Delphim's freckled hide.

If there was a problem—and he'd never known the army not to have a problem—it was that he'd never expected to be called out for something like this; to be honest, he wasn't entirely comfortable with the situation.

Gander Pond was his hometown.

These were his people.

Yet his orders could not have been more specific: *Secure the mountain, seal the perimeter, let no one past. No one. If anyone tries, shoot to kill.*

They wouldn't tell him what had happened, but the scuttlebutt was that some top-secret aircraft had crashed on the summit on its way to Colorado from Ohio. Which figured. And if things were bad enough, what with the first of the damned tourists already whooping and hollering up the road, any minute now he knew he was going to be swamped by brass from every service, inundated by conflicting orders, and sooner or later told to take his men up. Probably to recover the bodies.

He shuddered.

He hated bodies.

He had nightmares about bodies, saw bodies in his daydreams, and every time he spotted someone napping he wanted to scream.

Nevertheless, he was, first and foremost, a soldier in this man's army.

He knew his duty—let someone else take care of the goddamn bodies.

Adjusting his shoulders, steeling his gaze, he examined the lineup before him as best he could without moving. The first car bulged oddly at the top and was obviously in need of serious destruction; the one behind it was red, a made-for-speed convertible with a powerful-looking man driving and an obviously classy dame in the passenger seat whom he was sure he had seen somewhere before; the third wasn't a car at all, but an overweight palomino with a braided mane and tail. He squinted. There were two riders—the first was a cud-chewing cowboy in a baseball cap, and behind him, for god's sake, was that damned Chinaman, the one married to the bigmouth with the mustache back in town. Ranged behind them were at least a half dozen other cars with heads poking out the windows.

The horse pranced in place.

Down the line, someone blew an impatient horn.

A situation, Wagoneer thought glumly; Lord, we got us a stupid situation here.

"Hey, Sarge, you want a warning shot or something?"

He glared back at Private Delphim, then marched to the lead car, moved to the driver's side, and leaned over. "You want to tell me what you're doing here, sir?" he asked politely, his voice loud enough to carry down the row without deafening the driver.

A handsome man some ten years younger than his own mid to late forties poked his head out the window, and Wagoneer was instantly struck by the impression that he knew this guy, or that he'd at least seen him before. Several times. Impossible. The man wasn't one of Gander's homegrown. Yet Wagoneer couldn't help believing that he'd seen this dude somewhere before.

"Sir, please state your business here. This is a restricted area."

"The mountain blew up," the man said.

An accent, he thought; Christ, the guy's a foreigner.

"I can see that, sir."

The man shrugged. "We were curious."

Spy, Wagoneer thought immediately; damn, the guy might be a spy.

He peered deeper into the car and saw a woman seated beside him. Dark-skinned. Clearly Hispanic. Great; they were both foreigners.

"Would it be possible," the man said, "to have a look?"

"Well, sir, I'm sorry, sir, but no. In fact, I think it would be better if perhaps you and the young lady turned around and went back where you came from."

The man smiled. "I understand completely. But could you perhaps tell me what happened up there?"

Wagoneer risked ambush annihilation by holstering his weapon to assume his omniscient, authoritarian stance. Spies or not, foreigners or not, he didn't think he had to worry about someone who drove a neon-red car with antlers on the roof. Unless the guy planned to gore him to death.

"Sir, I'm afraid that's classified at the moment."

The woman muttered something.

"Excuse me," the foreigner said politely, pulled his head in, and snapped, "What?"

The woman made no attempt to keep her voice down or disguise the suspicion in it. "How come they got here so fast?" She gestured at the barricade and the men behind it. "We weren't that long getting here. How come?"

"I'm sure I don't know, my dear." Then he looked back at Wagoneer, who kept his expression admirably bland. "Sergeant, could you at least tell me if anyone is injured? I know a smattering of first aid. Perhaps I could be of some assistance."

"Thank you very much for your offer, sir," Wagoneer replied, "but we have matters well in hand. Now please," and he waved them gone.

"Ask him how they got here so fast!" the woman demanded.

The sergeant, who had had no small experience with wives and angry sweethearts, smiled. "Because, ma'am, we're trained to respond to emergencies in the fastest possible manner." His smile broadened. "It's our job."

The woman, who was not, in the usual scheme of secret missions in the mountains in New Jersey, all that bad in a physical sort of way, returned the smile so coldly he almost shivered. "Crock and bull, man. You knew the plane was gonna crash, didn't you?"

Wagoneer stiffened and backed off a step. "Sir, I really must insist."

"Right." The man nodded sharply and made an impossibly awkward U-turn that nearly caught the sergeant on the shoulder with one horn. Then he was gone, but Wagoneer didn't move until the taillights were well out of sight.

The second car followed without having to be told.

The palomino reared, whickered, and vanished.

The rest were like sheep, and soon the road was dark and empty again.

"Hey, Sarge!" Ham called from behind the lines.

Wagoneer rubbed his chin thoughtfully.

"Sarge, someone on the radio for you!"

He would remember that face. The man's too. There was something about them he didn't quite trust, and he reminded himself to request more men for guard duty. He had a strange and not unfamiliar feeling that this was going to be a long, very long night.

"Sarge, it's the White House!"

Sure, Wagoneer thought, and I'm the little fucking house on the prairie.

But, five minutes later, when he handed the radio back, his rugged face was pale, his Adam's apple bobbed, and a fluttering began in his stomach that no amount of instant Beret Zen could settle.

"Sarge?"

He took a deep breath.

"Hey, Sarge, you okay?"

He exhaled very slowly.

"Sarge, look, why don't you sit down for a minute, huh? Ain't nothing happening now anyway. Why don't you take five?"

Wagoneer looked to the youngster and clamped a hand on his scrawny shoulder. "Boy," he said, "you got folks at home?"

Delphim nodded eagerly. "Yep, sure do. Mom, Pop, two kid brothers, and a baby sister."

The sergeant cleared his throat. "Son," he said huskily, "if you ever tell me it's the White House on the line when it's really the White House and I don't believe you because you are one sorry son of a bitch again, your kin are gonna be orphans."

Delphim looked to his buddies, who studiously examined the purple sky for signs of invading Mongols; then he looked back and said, "But Sarge, it *was* the White House. They said it was."

"I know." He was weary. Unaccountably and bone-deep weary. "I know."

"So what did they say?"

Wagoneer looked to the top of Gander Mountain and pointed. "Come dawn, we're going up there."

"Holy shit."

"And I'll tell you the truth, son . . . I don't think we're coming back."

Delphim and the others fell silent for several minutes, before the private closed one eye and said, "So who's gonna ride in the tank?"

It didn't take long for John Smith to realize that he was more lost now then he was when he'd awakened after the patrol car's crash. The thought didn't frighten him. At least whatever it was that had started to chase him was gone now, crashing past without stopping.

He didn't know what it was.

He was not the slightest bit curious.

For in the fading purple glow, as he had thrown himself desperately to one side in frantic hope of finding safety and a fortuitous unoccupied large hole, he could have sworn he saw what resembled slime-covered scales on a massive green appendage that batted aside a pine tree as if it were made of flimsy cardboard.

It was, of course, his terror that had distorted what he thought he saw.

It was hunger, mayo gone bad, that had given him unto the hands of unrestrained hallucinations.

And it was another venerable pine that, as he raced head-long through the underbrush, stopped him cold.

He didn't mind.

As consciousness crept away as on the gentle pads of a stealthy chipmunk escaping from a voracious hawk, he knew that lying on the ground this night was the second wisest thing he'd ever done in his life.

And that Fate, for whatever reason, had other plans for him.

For now, however, he was grateful that he didn't have to listen to Twiller's goddamned moaning.

Something big moved through the trees.

Benny Hart, pinned under a smoldering branch that had fallen across his legs, froze in his attempts to extricate himself. He prayed. He shut his eyes tightly so that he wouldn't have to see the grizzly lumber into the clearing just prior to ripping out his throat.

He waited.

And when, hundreds of years later, the sound and the Kodiak passed, and there was nothing left but the comforting sounds of a potential forest fire, he nearly wept in gratitude.

Get a grip on yourself, he ordered then; stop farting around and take hold!

He did, and took stock as well.

His ears were stoppered, his chest ached with the effort to breathe the smoky air, his arms had been lacerated, his spine bruised all to hell and gone. Yet he fought that enveloping branch until he was free, fought through the minor but debilitating pain until he regained his feet, fought through the smoke until he found MaryLou's body lying against a blackened boulder.

"Oh my goodness," he said, and knelt beside her. He brushed the hair from her face, slapped her cheeks lightly, placed a palm against her chest to see if she was breathing.

"Oh lord," he said.

He could detect no signs of life.

"Oh damn," he swore because he thought it was appropriate, and wondered if he could find any of her gold before the woods burned down on his head.

Not far beyond the roadblock, just a few yards around the turn, the Holy Spirit Today Tabernacle Society limousine pulled off the road onto a narrow trail. Ten yards in, it stopped. The engine stopped. The brake lights winked out. The headlamps fluttered out. The only sound now was the creak and ping of cooling metal.

IT was unhappy, and uncharacteristically confused.

Despite ITs highly evolved night vision and near sonarlike hearing, IT had been unable to locate and destroy that which had threatened ITs very existence on this alien planet. IT didn't like that very much, and attributed the unusual failing of ITs combat-trained senses to unforeseen residual effects of the crash. But that shouldn't have been. IT was an organism of such high sophistication that nothing in the universe, much less the solar system, should have thrown ITs inner systems off.

Everything was foreseen where IT was concerned, including what happened after IT crashed.

For a long minute, IT paused in ITs angry charge, testing the air, sifting through the sounds of the unnatural night.

For a long minute, IT strained every nontactile faculty IT had, probing, cataloging, challenging ITself to find an answer where, it seemed, one did not exist.

Then IT heard the growing rumble of primitive fossil-fuel engines, and IT knew instantly what they were. IT had not studied the ethereal transmissions for nothing all these decades.

IT moved forward stealthily, unnervingly so for a thing of ITs size, little more now than a nightmare's shadow.

The rumbling stopped and was soon replaced by an unpleasant chittering that made ITs aural organs twitch.

A dozen yards more, and IT parted a thick, needle-laden branch and saw a gathering of creatures along the side of a black artificial pathway. IT grunted ITs satisfaction—they were communicating. And, to ITs surprise, in their midst was still another creature, this one so unlike the others that IT was momentarily puzzled.

Until knowledge blossomed, and IT nodded.

A horse, IT thought, is a horse. Of course!

And though IT had nothing against the equine beast of burden, IT knew that, at last, it was time to stop hiding.

Kent rounded the first bend, checked his rearview mirror to be sure the soldiers were out of sight, then lifted his foot from the accelerator and drifted another fifty yards before pulling over onto the shoulder.

"What?" Chita demanded.

He said nothing, eloquently. He only opened his door and slid outside, folded his arms across his chest, and leaned back against the Dilemma.

He looked at Gander Mountain, its purple-and-black-shadowed slope looming directly in front of him; he looked up the road as a pair of bright headlights swept down upon him; he looked back at the mountain and at the fan-shaped glow that seemed to fade even as he watched.

A muffled explosion didn't startle him.

A scuttling possum didn't faze him.

The headlights pinned him, passed him, and a low-slung automobile he would kill for if he could get the antlers on it pulled off in front of his own vehicle with a protest of brakes and a downshift worthy of James Bond.

Chita came around the back to stand beside him. "You got a plan, Lord?"

"I'm not a lord."

"Of course you're not," a baritone responded genially. "You're a baron." A tanned and horridly dressed young man held out his hand in greeting. "You're Kent Montana, aren't you? The television and movie star?"

"Movies?" Chita said.

Kent smiled modestly as he shook the hand. "Indeed I am. And you are . . . ?"

"Hooker," Chita muttered as an equally blonde and barely disheveled woman hurried up to join them.

"Exactly," the man said with a delighted grin. He shook Chita's startled hand. "Nicodemus Hooker." He nodded toward the mountain. "I was curious."

"And I," Kent admitted.

A palomino slowed to a canter as it came abreast of them, and Artie Chong dropped nimbly off the back of the saddle, staggered a few paces, then grinned broadly as he approached the group. The horse's rider tethered the nervous animal to a shrub just beyond the sports car.

Kent greeted the Oriental warmly, Chita sneered, and the others introduced themselves, all the while keeping their gazes on the glow in the sky.

When the palomino's rider joined them, Art said, "American friends, and m'lord, this is Mr. Ex Player. A close friend of the family. I hitched a ride on his magnificent beast, which he calls, very quaintly, Trigger Too."

Kent, having never seen a real-life East Coast cowboy before, studied the newcomer closely. Player was an extremely lank man, poorly shaven, coarse spikes of sandy hair frantically trying to escape from beneath his backward-turned baseball cap. He chewed either gum or tobacco with insolent serenity; he wore gold-piped coveralls, dusty boots, rawhide gloves, and a red bandanna around his neck.

"Meetcha," he said laconically, wiping his hand on his hip before offering it all around.

The palomino pawed the ground.

Player told it to get stuffed.

Kent watched the rest of the traffic go by, some of the vehicles slowing, none of them stopping as they headed back to town with the news of the army's entrenchment on Mountain Road. As he did, he heard the Jersey cowpoke explain that he had been christened Extra because his mother, rest her soul, had conned the local newspaper editor into printing a special edition announcing his birth. Casopia thought it was cute and heartwarming; Chita rolled her eyes.

Then Hooker shifted to stand on Kent's left.

"Sure looks like something crashed up there, all right."

"Yep."

"I doubt it was a plane."

Kent nodded his agreement. "I am beginning to wonder myself." He watched as Ex showed Casopia the proper way to bite off a chaw without messing up the coverall bib. "Yet what else can it be?"

"Alien," Hooker whispered.

Jesus, Kent thought in a moment of panic, the man's from Immigration. He immediately composed a letter of indignation to his mother and eased nervously to his right, bumping into Chita, who was explaining to Chong why she hadn't shown up for work that night. That it was her night off didn't seem to impress the cook. He shook a scolding finger at her and mumbled something about a wok on the wild side of the rice menu.

Kent thought he heard something moving in the woods across the road, but no one else seemed to notice, so he switched his attention back to the man in the yellow shirt and lavender sport coat.

"Alien," the scientist whispered again.

"I heard you the first time," Kent snapped.

Hooker looked at him, puzzled. "My goodness, have I offended you in some way? I know stars of your magnitude are sensitive, but I can't see—"

The unmistakable beat of rotors interrupted him, and they looked up just as a helicopter soared over the forest at their back, banked, and flew north around the bend. It hovered. It dropped slowly out of sight. Two more quickly followed, these low enough for Kent to realize they were troop carriers.

His eyes widened briefly.

"Well," Hooker said, "reinforcements, it would seem." He chuckled. "Aliens."

Kent glared at him and restudied the road, his mind on a high-speed search for a satisfactory explanation. This whole thing was most unusual. He pondered the grizzled sergeant's true motives in hustling them away. A top-secret plane or missile was the logical answer, yet right next to him was an official from Immigration. Yet again, one didn't call out the army just to haul a minor baron back to his native island so his mother could cop the family fortune.

It didn't make sense.

Unless . . .

He snapped his fingers.

"Aliens!" he blurted.

"Precisely," Hooker replied smugly. "No plane in existence crashes purple." He nodded toward the roadblock. "And they certainly don't need a full company of soldiers to mount a rescue attempt."

Chita smacked Kent's shoulder. "Told you, gringo. Give the waitress some credit, okay?"

"You have it," he answered magnanimously.

Ex burst into raucous laughter when Casopia choked on a nibble of his chaw.

Chong, meanwhile, positioned himself on the road's center white line, brushed fastidiously at his frock coat, and stood with hands on hips, facing the curve around which they'd just come, and the choppers had just gone. "I do not have confidence in the men with guns who come out of nowhere," he announced with a shake of his head. "A hurtful bang of unknown origin destroys my pitiful business and distresses my humble wife, my streets are disgracefully littered with human debris, many Americans are in a panic, and instead of the soldiers marching and flying into our fair city in order to assist us, they stay out here." He shook his head again. "I am not trustful of them."

Kent agreed with a grunt.

"I think," Hooker said, "we may be dealing with something quite extraordinary here."

"Aliens," Kent repeated.

"It's not without the realm of possibility."

He still had difficulty crediting it. The unnatural glow could easily have been made by some new type of fuel, or burning alloy, or any one of a dozen different things. Aliens, men from Mars, little green men, things with tentacles and teeth, were just not in the cards.

Still, there were all those soldiers—

A sudden thrashing crashing midway up the slope disrupted his pondering.

Chita grabbed his hand.

Chong wasted no time leaping from the road to the safety of Kent's car, lifting himself to the roof so that he might peer through the antlers.

Casopia hustled to the scientist's side and snared his arm tightly enough to cause the man to wince.

"I think," Hooker said, "something is out there."

"It might just be a tree coming down, or a rock," Kent suggested. "Surely the fire that's raging up there could have caused such a fall."

The cowboy shook his head at them in disgust. "Nambies," he said, and spit. "Ain't none of you never heard a critter making tracks in the woods before?"

None of them responded.

The cowboy snorted. "Didn't think so." He took off his cap, slapped it against his leg, jammed it back on. "Lordy, you let a bunch of sissy boys in fancy fatigues drive you off, ain't no wonder a stupid squirrel's gonna make you wet your pants."

"Here now," Hooker protested, drawing an offended Casopia closer. "There's no call for that sort of language with ladies present."

The cowboy tipped his cap in apology. Then he walked back to his mount, reached into a sheath on the far side, and pulled out a shotgun he broke open and loaded with shells from a coverall pocket.

"Big man," Chita said derisively. "You always take on killer squirrels with that?"

"Never hurts to be careful," Player told her with a quick practice sighting down the stock of his weapon. "Might be a bear. Might be a bobcat. Might be a cougar."

"And what," Kent wanted to know, "if it's a human being? What then?"

"Well, Jesus on a wagonwheel, man, you think I'm gonna shoot first and ask questions later?" He spat. He wiped his mouth. "Son of a bitch, you actors are all alike."

"Actor?" said Casopia.

"Sure," the man said, marching out onto the road. "Ain't you never seen *Passions and Power*?"

Kent felt a blush coming on.

"Guy's an Irish butler."

"English!" he corrected heatedly.

"Thought you was from Scotland," Chita said.

"I am."

"But you just said you were English."

"On television I am English," he explained. "In real life, I am a Scot."

"Wow," she said. "Takes some acting, huh?"

"Damn right."

"Have you ever been in the movies?" Casopia asked.

There was no time for an answer.

The cowboy reached the other side of the road, snapped the shotgun closed with a jerk of arm and wrist, and called, "Hey in there! You got two legs, you'd best come out now, afore you git hurt. I got a gun here, I can use it."

"Swell," Chita muttered.

The crashing continued.

Chong slid off the roof and peered through the window.

Hooker nervously jingled his keys in his hand.

"Mr. Player," Kent called, "I think you'd better wait back here. Let the army handle it."

The cowboy spat derisively over his shoulder. "Hey!" he called into the forest devoid of light except for the purple on top of the mountain. "Your last chance coming up."

Out of the purple blackness, a fifty-foot tree fell onto the highway.

Chong raced to the palomino, leapt into the saddle, and was gone before he had a chance to grab the reins.

Chita suggested to no one in particular that no bear in these stinking woods could knock down a perfectly good tree and didn't Kent think it was time to leave these things to those half-assed soldiers?

The cowboy brought the shotgun to his shoulder.

Hooker brought Casopia to his car and eased her in, reached over, and slipped his key into the ignition. He turned it on. He stood by the driver's door.

A muggy wind carried an odor out of the forest—the stench of sweat and blood and charred flesh and burning bones and things which had no names that walked the night in foreign climes.

Chita gagged.

Kent took a step onto the blacktop. "Mr. Player, I must insist that you—"

Another tree fell.

The cowboy fired.

And something most definitely not a bear screamed in the forest.

"Oh shit," Kent said.

The cowboy fired again.

And Kent said, "Oh lord," when something reached out of the trees and yanked off the cowboy's head.

~II~

The Plot

◆ 1 ◆

Master Sergeant Wagoneer was well aware of the awe with which his men watched the three Chinooks circle their position, engines roaring like angry wasps, spotlights nailing first the roadblock, then the tank, then him, before they landed in a neat line on the road, their blades just barely missing the reach of the flanking trees. He did not turn away from the fierce wash of air. He did not lower the M-16 Delphim had handed to him on command. And he did not flinch when he saw scores of men leap from the doors and take up defensive positions along the shoulder.

Inside, however, he was both annoyed and disturbed.

He was annoyed because someone higher up had obviously decided that this assignment was too important to be handled by a mere master sergeant. That meant officers. And that meant petty bullshit, regulations, uniform inspections, and a lot of running around in the dark.

He managed to sigh without making a sound.

It also meant that he wasn't going to have until dawn to figure out a way to avoid going up that damned mountain.

"Hey, Sarge, you think it's the President?"

Wagoneer admired himself for avoiding the death penalty. He only shook his head once, and stepped in front of the roadblock, waiting for the officer in charge of this impressive display in the middle of nowhere with no one to see it to get the hell out of the lead chopper and get this show on the road. Or wherever.

"Hey, Sarge, maybe it's a general."

A tap on his right arm. He looked down to see a hard-muscled Brooklyn Greek push his combat helmet back on his head.

"Sarge," said Milos Athnos, "you don't think it could be good old Ironass, do you?"

Wagoneer smiled without humor. He and Milos had spent many a lonely night on Arctic guard duty, in jungle skirmishes, in desert skirmishes, in urban skirmishes, and in skirmishes in bars over the same woman. Athnos was still a corporal. The guy liked it that way. The big lunk.

"Bite your tongue," he said.

"Could happen, y'know."

"Really?" Delphim said from his left. "You really think the major will be here?"

"Kid," said Athnos, "in this man's army, you always expect the unexpected."

"Wow," Delphim said.

And Wagoneer said, in quite a different tone, "Wow," when a dark figure clambered out of the first chopper, signaled to the pilot, and stood back as the three dark birds rose into the night. "Son of a bitch."

Athnos said, "Oh shit," and slipped back into the ranks.

Suddenly there were gunshots.

Bolts were snapped back, the tank's engines ground into action, and the soldiers on the shoulder dropped in place and aimed at each other across the road.

There was a faint scream from around the bend.

There was an unearthly bellow.

Instantly Wagoneer spun around, snapped orders that had a dozen men removing the sawhorses to make room for the tank, the rest lining up in two ranks he led off in a trot toward the sound of yet another animal-like cry.

Along the way, he ordered the men in the road to fall in. They did, without question, and pride in his authority swelled his chest long enough to keep him from sagging when he came abreast of the officer waiting for him on the center line.

"Sergeant," clipped Major Ironass Settbach.

"Evening, Major," he said, belts clinking, boots thumping. "Nice night for a whatever."

Settbach agreed with a noncommittal grunt, checked to be

sure the small army was in proper formation, then pulled out a decidedly nonregulation Uzi machine pistol and rammed its clip home with an expert smack.

"You want to tell me what's going on?" Wagoneer asked, turning to trot backward to check on his men.

"Top secret, Sergeant," the major said.

"Shit."

"Perhaps, but that's the way the general wants it."

He sneered. It was safe to sneer with the major. The major wanted to forget about colonel and go right to general. There was precedent. The major evidently had every intention of using this incident to follow up on that. Wagoneer didn't mind. As long as when the major made general, the general didn't forget who had helped the major when the major was still a major.

The crash of a tree.

"Sounds big," the major said.

Wagoneer nodded. Delphim rode up in a Jeep. The major instantly leapt in beside the driver, and Wagoneer scrambled into the back. This was the part he liked. He hated trotting in full combat gear. Riding was much better. You didn't see so many bodies this way.

"Pop a light!" he ordered.

Behind him, someone obeyed, and the hiss of the flare's ascent was soon followed by a bright yellow glare and momentarily banished the old purple shadows and replaced them with new ones that writhed and angled as the light drifted toward the ground.

They rounded the bend.

Wagoneer was nearly thrown into the major's lap when Delphim slammed on the brakes and said, "Holy shit!"

And the sergeant saw the body on the road. The body's head lying next to it. The limousine.

And the *Thing* that straddled the blood-spattered white line.

"Well," the major said with admirable calm, "talk about your ugly."

IT snarled.

IT screamed.

IT had tasted blood, and IT was pleased.

• • •

"Permission to fire, Major," said Master Sergeant Wagoneer.

The major stood up in the front seat and put the Uzi on full automatic. "Don't waste time, Sergeant," the major answered. "Dead majors don't collect pensions. Dead sergeants don't either."

Wagoneer raised his hand.

The sound of a hundred weapons being readied.

"Sarge, wait!" said Ham Delphim, voice hushed with fear and dread. "Aren't we supposed to try to contact it first or something?"

The major stared at him in stunned disbelief.

"Maybe all it wants is peace."

Wagoneer hesitated.

The major turned around and said, "Sergeant, do your duty."

"Sarge, please!"

He lowered his hand sharply.

He hoped to hell his men fired high enough not to hit that stupid limousine.

"The Lord is my shepherd," intoned Phil Lager.

"My seat belt's stuck," Phyllis complained.

"I shall not want."

"Damnit, the buckle's jammed again."

"He maketh me to lie down beside still waters."

"Shit. Smack this with the Good Book, Phil. I get shot in the Tabernacle limo by those trigger-happy troopers, it isn't going to look right."

"He restoreth my soul."

"Philip!"

"He leadeth me not into temptation."

"Damn. There go the tires."

For the first swift and terrifying mile, Kent steadfastly refused to pay heed to anything Chita had to say to him. At the top of her well-oiled and outwardly tanned lungs. He was too busy trying to hold the Dilemma on the road, prevent Chong from running over him with the palomino, and at the same time signal to Hooker, who probably wasn't with Immigration after all, that they should meet somewhere, and damned soon, to figure out exactly what it was they had seen snatch and jerk the rural cowboy and his head into the woods.

He was shaken.

Images of slavering beasts and slobbering beasties whirled through his mind as he fought to control the burgeoning panic and terror that struggled for possession of his already none too steady faculties.

Fear that the *Thing* would follow kept his gaze as much on the rearview mirror as on the road ahead. If it did follow, he knew they wouldn't have a prayer of survival.

A flare popped overhead, and Chita's bursts of unintelligible Spanish switched into imaginative Anglo-Saxon obscenities that threatened to turn his ginger hair red with their heat.

His right foot kept sliding off the accelerator, his left hand was slick with cold perspiration and kept slipping around the beveled steering wheel, and his right hand several times had to reluctantly slap Chita to prevent her, in time-honored heroic fashion, from disintegrating into a useless quivering mass before his very eyes or, as he thought about it, in his peripheral vision, since the Pagoda's chief chef was once again attempting to turn the palomino into a short-range flyer.

At long last, she calmed her volatile Hispanic hysteria and slugged him instead.

The car veered to the left.

She slugged him again.

The swerving car nearly sideswiped Chong and the golden horse into a ditch.

He slapped her again without hesitation.

She demanded to be released from this speeding death trap so she could walk home and see the rest of her movie. Preferably alone.

"Chita," he said, "you are not yourself."

"The hell," she answered angrily, and opened the door.

With one hand on the wheel, he lunged across her lap for the handle, yanked the door shut, and, as he straightened, took firm hold of her hands as he brought the Dilemma off the verge and back onto the blacktop. "You must be calm!" he commanded. "For all our sakes, Chita, you must be strong!"

Gunfire erupted behind them, along with the sound of the tank's booming cannon.

She burst into tears.

Kent swallowed hard and braced himself for the concussion that never came.

The forest blurred past them. They were not dark, however, because a fire storm of flares had ignited above them, and the hellish light was, he thought, like a dawn too soon come for the comfort of the world.

His mother was beginning to look pretty damn tame by now.

Chita, her eyes still leaking angry tears, leaned over the back seat. "I don't see nothing."

"Thank God."

The highway curved again and widened, the trees backed away, and he could see the dim glow of Gander Pond beyond the dark silhouette of Gander Palace. Some of the electricity must have been restored, he guessed. God help them when they learn that far worse is in their future.

He frowned.

What the hell kind of way was that for a butler to talk? In the middle of an unbelievable crisis. On the other hand, *excuse me, madam, but Armageddon is served* didn't exactly read like *Troilus and Cressida* either. Come to think of it, nothing did. And it was evident that he was in danger of losing control again, because he never thought about Shakespeare unless he was having nightmares.

There were very few butlers in Shakespeare.

The gunfire doubled, redoubled, then abruptly faded.

Ahead, Hooker veered without braking into the Palace's empty parking lot while Casopia knelt precariously on her seat and gestured frantically for the rest of them to follow.

Kent did so immediately, despite Chita's demand that they continue on to Indiana.

Artie Chong, frock coat flapping, hair streaming, mouth open in either a shout of encouragement or a prolonged silent scream, valiantly attempted to turn the speeding palomino, which would have none of it. It galloped on, and was soon swallowed by the dark.

By the time Kent had braked and parked, Hooker and Casopia were already on the blacktop, waiting anxiously.

Chita dried her eyes with the bottom of her shirt.

"I'm very sorry," Kent said as the engine whined down and silence filled the car. "I didn't mean to hurt you."

"That's all right." She winked. "I didn't mean to hurt you."

The night was quiet.

His smile was tender.

"You know, under other circumstances, with less danger around us, I might be tempted to ask you out to dinner again. Asking again, that is. We haven't had dinner yet because you didn't like the bit about the nuns."

On the third-floor balcony, a portly old man with a neatly trimmed white beard and a green felt Tyrolean hat began to play a trumpet with a sweetness and dour melancholy that reminded Kent of dew on the heather and sheep on the hills. On the second floor, a skinny old woman in a sombrero ringed with wax grapes joined in with a counterpoint twelve-string guitar. On the first, a muted violin played by a red-faced old man in an argyle cardigan. The incongruous music they created on this evening of alien terror was undeniably beautiful, haunting in the spectral light that fell over the small community.

Kent leaned forward, the better to see the unlikely trio through his bug-spattered windshield. "I shall hear that song for the rest of my life," he whispered.

"Our song," she whispered, leaning forward too, her left hand drifting to his thigh.

He felt the heat of her cheek, saw a glint of moisture on her lips. "I do believe they sense that this is their last chance to play together."

Her fingers tightened ever so slightly. "And what about us, Baron? Do you think we'll ever roll our *r*'s together again?"

He looked over at her and covered her hand with his. He did not understand the feeling that came over him with the suddenness of an unexpected royal fanfare, that cast butterflies into the soaring sky of his abdomen, that buoyed the rolling sea of his chest cavity, that made him want to cast away his fear and giggle like a schoolchild confronted with Father Christmas. It was, to be classically understated, wildly inappropriate. It might even be blasphemous. Some *Thing* had viciously snuffed out an innocent life before his very eyes; some *creature* had torn a human being asunder before he had been able to lift a finger to help; some nightmarish *alien* monstrosity had shaken the ancestral foundations of his belief in the centricity of man in the universe, perhaps for all time; and here he was, gazing into the limpid, yet vibrant, brown eyes of a saucy little wench in a car with antlers welded to the roof.

Love, he thought; love is strange.

"Chita," he began, and was hushed with a finger that brushed across his lips.

She gave him a sad smile. "I don't think it's right for us just now, Kent."

His own smile was melancholic. "Alas, I was just thinking that very same thing."

Silently, then, in this inexplicable parking lot oasis, they exchanged the words neither of them had had the courage to say to each other before this cherished moment. Then, as horn, violin, and guitar reached the climax of their post-alien invasion chorus of lament and ultimate hope, they exchanged a chaste and thoroughly unsatisfying kiss, which might, had Kent had anything to say about it and the hell with *things* and *creatures* and bloody damn *aliens*, have turned into something more akin to more satisfying lust had not Hooker knocked on the windshield and grinned at them.

"Excuse me for interrupting," he said, coming around to the window, "but don't you think we should, as one of my more earnest colleagues might say, get this show on the road?"

Chita glared at him. "You a virgin or what?"

Hooker backed away, flustered.

"Don't mind him," she said to Kent as he opened the door. "He got the name, he just don't have the game." She reached for his arm. "You were saying?"

Regrettably Kent's well-honed inner sense of timing warned him that the outer time—and with it, the baser opportunity—had passed. Many things had to be done quickly, matters worked out, plans made, and theories discussed before anything significant would happen between them again. Chita nodded understandingly when he explained and apologized. He blew her a kiss, a promise, a dream; she trapped it in her hand and pressed it to her cheek, closed her eyes, and sighed when the horn player fell into the shrubs and began snoring.

Then: "Right," Kent said decisively, stepping out of the car. "The first thing we must do is notify the authorities before this gets out of hand."

"I think," Casopia said, "the army already knows by now."

She cocked her head meaningfully.

He listened to the dread sound of accelerated gunfire. "Then we must warn the town."

At that very second, it seemed as if every fire, air-raid, and boating-accident siren in the valley had been turned on simultaneously.

"Well done, Artie," he said with verbal applause.

He glanced around the parking lot, ignoring for the moment the efforts of the violinist and guitarist to get their somnolent friend unstuck from a wood chip mound. The gunfire had abruptly ceased once more. A lone flare burned radiantly against the sky. The purple glow pulsed and settled lower against the silhouetted treetops. All were noted with an intelligent nod, and he wondered what a good butler would do at a time like this. Canapés were out of the question. If he were home, on the other hand, and dodging his mother and her hired Highland assassins, he would undoubtedly invite his guests into the sitting room, where, over brandy and a tray of sweets, they might feed each other's imaginations until they were able to solve the current problem.

Which was, at the moment, somewhat undefined.

Hooker tapped his arm. "Maybe we ought to try to contact whatever is out there."

Casopia tapped his arm in turn, rather hard, Kent thought as Hooker yelped and danced away. "Contact? You mean as in 'Hi, sailor, new in town' contact? Are you nuts, Nick? Some guy just lost his head out there!"

"Some *guy*," Hooker reminded her stiffly, "had just unloaded both barrels of a shotgun at it. I'd be annoyed too if it happened to me."

"You'd be dead," she retorted.

"Yes, but—"

"It had wings," Chita said with a shiver.

"Well, I'm not so sure about that," Kent said in gentle contradiction. "Though I'm fairly positive I saw two pairs of giant, faceted eyeballs."

"Surely not," Hooker disagreed. "The head was much too small."

"Small?" Casopia yelped. "It was twice as big as a house, for Christ's sake!"

"The head?"

"The *Thing*," she said in disgust. "And it had four purple arms, not wings."

Kent frowned as he settled one finger against his chin. He was almost positive he thought he had seen what might have been wings protruding mothlike from its shoulders. But if it wasn't moot at this point, it was certainly beside that very same point, since there was nothing they could do about it until they figured out what to do next.

The gunfire resumed without warning. Resounding, echoing booms this time, and a considerable amount of heavy small-arms fire.

"Kent," Chita said, her apprehensive gaze on the orange and gold flares drifting down upon the mountain, "I don't think we have much time."

"No offense, Major," said Master Sergeant Wagoneer from his position in the ditch, "but I know damned well we don't have much time."

Major Settbach glared at him, cheeks smudged with dirt, chin scratched all to hell and gone as a result of being thrown out of the Jeep when Private Delphim had panicked, threw the vehicle into reverse, and nearly smacked into the tank. Only a swift grab of the wheel by the sergeant had saved them. It had also put them in the ditch.

"If we don't stop that thing," the major called over the roar of gunfire, "it's going straight into that hick burg and smash it flat."

Wagoneer bristled at the slur on his hometown.

Settbach ignored his reaction, calling, "Is that thing ready yet?" to Delphim, who was under the hood.

The private pushed himself free and nodded as he dusted his hands on his fatigues. "Whenever you are, sir."

"Sergeant, a holding action is imperative here. Give me time to get into town and prepare the defenses."

He nodded, and called out to Private Fabian Lamanza to

stop combing his goddamn hair and at least pretend he was in the army.

Another Jeep barreled past them, and he lifted himself up on his elbows just in time to see the *Thing* slap it casually to one side. The driver bailed out. His seven rocket-launcher-toting passengers followed soon enough, and they all vanished into the trees as the *Thing* snarled at them.

Carnage on the road.

Fire burning on the shoulders.

Smoke in the air.

The stench of pyrotechnic death and destruction.

And in the midst of it all, half obscured by the fighting, was a white limousine.

Who the hell *are* those people? Wagoneer wondered. But whoever it was, it was a miracle that the *Thing* hadn't bothered with them; it was a miracle of another more perverse kind that they hadn't tried to escape their ready-made coffin; and it was Athnos, he saw with a startled curse, who was crawling along the road toward the limo, rifle strapped to his back, a grenade in each hand, a dagger in his teeth.

"Milos!" he shouted.

The major yanked him down so hard, he nearly dislocated his shoulder. "Fool, do you want it to see us?"

"But that's my buddy out there."

The major's head shook side to side. "It's too late now, Sergeant."

The major was right.

The *Thing* had spotted the corporal. The ground shook as it took a single step forward. The firing stopped as if on command. The *Thing* reached over the roof of the limousine. Athnos leapt to his feet, pulled the pins on both grenades, and heaved them expertly at the *Thing*'s lowering head. One struck the brow and exploded, the other exploded at the same time against its neck. The *Thing* reeled, bellowing in pain as it backed away. The men cheered. Athnos, however, wasted no precious time admiring his temporary handiwork, but raced to the passenger door and flung it open. A moment later a bearded man scrambled out, knocking the corporal aside.

The *Thing*, though still evidently dazed by the twin concussions, saw him.

The bearded man stood tall, head high, and lifted something into the air.

"What is it, Sarge?" Delphim asked.

"A Bible, trooper," Settbach answered. "Looks like we got a preacher out there, doing the Lord's work."

Fool, Wagoneer thought in grudging admiration.

Silence save for the dying hiss of a flare, the harsh breathing of the *Thing*, and Athnos grunting as he reached back into the car.

And the resonant baritone voice of the preacher: "Repent, you ugly twin of a misguided grizzly! Repent, and come to the Lord, Who forgives all sins, even out there on Mars!"

The *Thing* eyed him curiously.

Wagoneer held his breath.

The preacher took a bold step closer and brandished the Bible over his head. "Repent! Rejoice! Sing hallelujah, you fat-headed hedgehog! We love you! We do not want to harm you! We are not your enemies!"

Athnos, his torso swallowed by the car and one leg kicking, swore loudly.

The *Thing* rumbled deep in its throat.

"Fear not, for behold! I bring you glad tidings and this here Good Book, which shall be your salvation!"

Wagoneer noted that many of his men, including Delphim, had their eyes closed in supporting prayer. The major's rifle, however, was aimed at the *Thing*'s closest eyeball.

Silence.

Peace.

Athnos vanished into the limousine without a sound.

The preacher spread his arms. "We come in peace, you idiot offspring of a half-baked muskrat!"

The *Thing* bent forward.

"These people don't want to hurt you! They are only protecting their hearth and home! Just as you would, if you had someone ugly enough to marry you, you one-eyed toad from Hell! Repent! Rejoice! Redeem yourself in the peace and love of the Lamb!"

The driver's door of the limousine opened, and Wagoneer spotted two figures crawling on the ground, toward the woods. He sagged with relief. And stiffened when the *Thing* took a shuffling step toward the trees.

"Stop!" the preacher commanded.

The *Thing* stopped.

Be damned, the sergeant thought.

"You do not want to kill them!" the preacher said, his voice almost singing. "We don't want to kill you! Nobody hereabouts wants to kill anybody!" A fist thumped the Bible. "It says right here, you don't want to kill anybody!"

Laboriously the *Thing* swung around.

"You gonna go against the Bible, you half-baked little god-forsaken critter what God loves anyway? You gonna defy the Word of the Everlasting Lord, you buck-toothed beaver?"

The *Thing* rumbled again.

The preacher stepped back uncertainly.

Wagoneer exchanged puzzled looks with the major.

"Did that thing say what I thought it said?" the major asked, clearly not wanting confirmation.

Delphim opened one eye.

Wagoneer stood, grenade launcher in one hand, pouch of ammunition slung over his shoulder. He scanned the embankment beyond the ditch. Athnos was gone.

"Say . . . what?" the preacher asked.

And the *Thing* sneered, "You betchum, Red Ryder," before a beam of intense red light shot from some orifice or other and fried the preacher where he stood.

"Thought so," said the major.

"Fire!" screamed Wagoneer, and launched his first volley.

It had seemed, for a few minutes, that Chita was amiss in her assessment of time remaining. A long silence had followed her ominous pronouncement, and Kent did his best to psychically prove her wrong without hurting her feelings.

Then the firing renewed itself with more vigor than before.

Nuts, he thought.

And was positive that from now events would move swiftly, barely giving him time to think, barely pausing long enough for him to take a breath, swirling about him like autumn leaves in a storm.

It was going to get confusing.

It was not going to be fun.

"My god, they're killing it!" Hooker lamented. "What a waste! What a damnable waste!"

Casopia cast a look at Kent that said *He can't help it, look at the way he dresses,* and led the shaken scientist away, toward the dubious sanctuary of the Gander Palace.

"Well, we sure can't stay here," Chita said after they left. "That army ain't army enough to keep that thing away." She stamped a foot. "Damn. You know, I could've stayed in Atlantic City. Great tips, great hours, great hunks, shit like that. For sure, no monsters come out of the water, except for the guys from Philadelphia that ain't seen the sun since 1927." She scratched her head vigorously. "Shit."

Suddenly Kent, struck by a mad impulse, grabbed her hands. "Get in the car."

"I can't."

"Why not?"

"You got my hands, man."

"So what? Get in the damned car!"

"Why?"

"Because," he said firmly, "we're getting away. I'm quite sure all the main roads have been blocked by now, since the army seems to have taken over in some fashion or other, but I'm just as sure we can find a fire trail, a deer path, something that will lead us out of the valley." He pulled her close. "I'll get you away from this, I swear it."

"No kidding?"

He smiled. "No kidding."

"And what about all those guys out there, shooting and dying and stuff?"

"That's what armies are for," he said, pulling her gently but urgently toward the Dilemma.

She resisted. "And what about the folks in town, huh? At the circus? In the campgrounds? In the lake? You think that's what they're for, you elitist baron with your hoity-toity castle and zillion servants?" She snapped her hands free. "You think little people like me are cannon fodder? You think we was born to take care of the likes of you, even to fighting things with big heads and disgusting private parts? You think that's all we're good for?"

He didn't know quite how to answer her.

On the one hand, that's precisely what he had been taught; on the other, he hadn't counted on coming across such a little spitfire as Chita Juarel. In fact, the closest he'd ever come to one was a muzzy photograph of his RAF father taken during World War II. And the women he had met equal to his supposed station had all previously been handpicked by his mother and valet. Even the nuns. And not a single one of them had ever rented, much less owned, a porn tape with such a tastefully eclectic musical background. Especially the nuns.

A Jeep sped past the parking lot.

A tank did its best to rumble close behind and was doing a pretty bad job of it.

He didn't count the women who had approached him while he'd been on *Passions and Power*. They were a different breed entirely, more concerned with asking him how to polish silver than make beds. It didn't matter that he was only acting; they either didn't believe it or didn't care, or believed it and thought he was lying through his perfectly capped teeth. Either way, hopping into the sack with a butler wasn't their idea of an afternoon with the help.

"What do you mean, private parts?" he asked at last.

Chita groaned, slapped her forehead, and stalked away.

He followed her, suddenly aware that he had once again transgressed some obscure American tribal custom, which got more confusing the more the country let foreigners in. At least, at home, he knew where he stood. Which was never, ever, with his back to his mother.

"Chita!"

"Go away!"

"Chita!"

She stopped and turned. "I told you go away. Now go away!"

"Please," he implored, "don't do this. Not now. We've still much to do before we get married."

Oh shit, he thought.

"Married?"

Hell's bells.

"Married?"

He gave her a modest shrug.

She gave him a slap that rang the fillings in his molars. "You think I can marry you, become one of the elitist baroness types and desert this place, these people, my forking job? You think I'm that kind of person?"

Jesus, he thought.

A shell exploded in the far corner of the parking lot. A tree splintered, rocks and dirt and bits of blacktop splattered the back of his head as the concussion thrust him into Chita's arms and they fell backward into the shrubs, his chin meeting her forehead with a responding crack.

"The tank," he gasped painfully. "It must be shooting at something."

Chita's response was muffled until he shifted his chest out of her face. "No shit" is what she said. "And that means the good guys ain't winning yet."

He stared at her; he felt her beneath him; he looked up and saw the geriatric trio staring back at him from the safety of the lobby. The song they played was spritely, slyly knowing, yet tinged with a hint of menace and impending doom. The horn player had a wood chip in one ear.

Hastily Kent pushed to his feet, pulled Chita up, and dusted them both off. "Well," he said, "I suppose I have no choice now."

"Good for you, Baron," she encouraged with a playful punch to his arm. "Stiff upper lip and all that."

"Oh hell, does it show?"

"A little ice, no sweat," she promised. "But now we gotta find out what's what, so we can figure out where we gotta do what we gotta do."

A shell blasted a chunk out of the corner of the west side of the building; a shrieking beam of red light melted in a smaller hole in the east side.

"Run!" he yelled, grabbing her arm. "For god's sake, run!"

He only hoped that they would make it, because something godawful big had just emerged from the dark and the smoke onto the highway.

· 2 ·

In a fit of unprecedented conscience that jarred with the credo of his liberation army, Benny Hart decided not to abandon the late MaryLou Krutch to the appetites of the ravenous creatures of the forest's purple-glow night.

That would be cruel; a mountain woman deserved better.

So, with as much care and reverence as he could, he slipped his hands under her arms and began the arduous task of dragging her body along the trail he'd discovered, figuring that her cabin was at the end of it. She would like that. Getting your bones picked clean by ants and beetles wasn't as romantic as it looked in the movies.

He sweated.

He strained.

Several times he was forced to detour around burning stumps and oddly crushed boulders.

Twice he attempted to carry her in his arms, and though he made good time while it lasted, his muscles were unequal to the task. And his nerves, at the onset of what sounded like World War III down on Mountain Road, deserted him altogether until he was able to round them up again with a stern speech and a few whacks across the temple.

He did not, however, leave MaryLou and investigate.

For which decision he was extremely glad when, without warning, he reached a very large clearing and saw the cabin. Actually it was a modest Victorian home made of stone, untreated logs, and adobe. From the outside, he guessed six rooms with a crawl-space attic and full basement. The rose garden was forty feet on a side. The porch was nearly hidden by relatively towering evergreen shrubs. The yard was spotted with large frames across which were stretched all manner of animal hides. A smokehouse squatted near the trees on the far side. A corral was next to it, but the condition of the fencing told him that the animals she kept there had long since broken free.

"Oh, MaryLou," he said quietly, shifting her once again into his arms. "You're home now."

She moaned softly.

He nearly dropped her.

Her eyelids flickered.

He staggered quickly to the porch and placed her on the ground by the steps.

The war continued, and clouds of smoke were blown through the clearing by an increasingly insistent wind.

"Not dead," he said in astonishment as he knelt beside her.

Damn, he thought uncharitably.

And within seconds, before his decently trained reflexes could stand him in good stead, he was lying down, on his back, her left hand on his throat, her right hand aiming the Bowie knife right at his chest.

"Hello, MaryLou," he said weakly.

"Goodbye, Hart," she told him as the blade sliced through his shirt above that very homonymic organ.

Frantically he shook his head in vehement denial at what she had obviously thought upon awakening and seeing them at her home, while, at the same time, he thought as fast as his extreme terror would permit. "Sweet MaryLou," he pleaded at last, his eyes filling with tears, "I'm so in love with you! Please, don't kill me."

The blade paused. Her eyes narrowed. "What's this love stuff? You get hit on the head or something?"

His lips quivered, his forehead glowed with perspiration, his stomach heaved, and his knee jerked as he sought for a word, a phrase, a brilliantly conceived lie that would get him the hell out of this mess.

Then she looked up, and his head twisted around, as a battered and bloodied figure staggered out of the trees.

"Jesus," she said, getting to her feet and dragging Benny up by the shirt front. "Who the hell are you?"

"John," the man said, coughing as he dropped heavily to his knees. "John Smith."

"Have it your way," she shrugged. "Out here in the mountains we don't care anyway, do we, army?"

Benny shook his head.

Gunfire ebbed and flowed far down the slope.

MaryLou scowled, released Benny's shirt, and said, "What the hell's going on down there?"

John Smith tried to speak, hacked, pointed to his throat, and Benny understood that he needed water, if not some esoteric medical attention the liberation army manual didn't cover. Quickly he hustled over to the well he had spotted on the other side of the rose garden, hauled up a wood bucket, unhooked it from its rope, hauled it back, and placed it in front of the stranger.

The man looked at it.

MaryLou disappeared into the house.

The man looked up at Benny. "You got a cup or something?"

MaryLou returned with a rifle.

"No," Benny snapped. "Now talk, Mr. Whoever You Are, or you don't get a drop."

The man plunged his head into the bucket.

"Nice," MaryLou said approvingly. "Torture him first, then listen to his story."

The man who called himself John Smith came up for air, licked his lips, and said, "Aliens."

"What?" MaryLou said.

"Aliens," the man repeated.

Benny scoffed. "C'mon, man, you think we're stupid or something?" He sneered. "Do you think we're really going to believe that the United States Army is down there on Mountain Road—in Gander Pond, yet—fighting with some kind of aliens from outer space?" He looked at MaryLou and laughed heartily. "You must think we're crazy!"

"I . . . saw one," the man gasped.

"No kidding," Benny said. "Wow."

"Benny," MaryLou cautioned.

"It was horrible," John Smith said, and attacked the bucket again.

"Benny, this is dumb," MaryLou said.

"Oh yeah?" he said. And reminded her about the crash, the purple light that still engulfed them and obviated the need for flashlights and torches, the strange sounds, the army, the guns, and the fact that if whatever had been in that spacecraft was down there now, fighting the damned army, then its spacecraft was all alone up here. Even if there was nothing left of it but pieces, those pieces would buy a hell of a big chunk of Gander Mountain once people knew what those pieces were, where they had come from, and how rare they were.

MaryLou looked at him with one eye closed. "How come you know all this stuff? You were up here with me."

"Because," he said, and tapped a finger to his temple. "Because."

"Yeah?"

He nodded.

Smith came up for air and said, "That son of a bitch was one ugly bastard."

MaryLou grinned and helped him to his feet. "You know where it is?"

Smith pointed downslope.

"No. I mean where it crashed. Do you know where it is?"

"Nope."

She grinned again.

Benny didn't like it.

"Come inside," she said. "We get you a change of clothes, something for that belly of yours, and then we'll talk about going up there and seeing what we can see."

"What?" Benny planted himself at the foot of the steps. "We can't wait! God, the place'll be overrun with tourists before we can blink. We gotta go now!"

"Go where?" asked Smith.

"To the flying saucer," MaryLou answered.

The man nodded sagely. "I see."

"You want to help?"

"MaryLou!"

Smith's expression suddenly became wary, switched to canny, shifted to blank. "What the hell," he said.

• • •

"Keep your disgusting hands off my thighs," Phyllis Lager whispered harshly.

"Lady, believe me, it ain't your thighs I'm interested in. I just grabbed them by mistake, that's all."

Phyllis lashed out with her foot and crawled on, seemingly for hours through a landscape more shadow than light, yet fearful that the demon from Hell that had taken her beloved Phil from her would soon turn its attention from swatting militant soldiers to raping and pillaging women.

"Lady, for god's sake, slow down!"

She paid the uncouth little person no heed. The farther away from the battlefield she could get, the better she would like it. Once safe, she would make her way back into town, write up the insurance claim for the limo, close down the Tabernacle, and beat her stockings out of here.

"Lady!"

A gritty hand gripped her waist.

She struggled, cried out, and a grimy hand clamped over her lips. Her eyes widened in fear and anger as a grizzled, swarthy face loomed into dim view.

"Damnit," the face spat, "it might hear you, you idiot!"

The tank fired a screaming round that echoed off the hills.

The hand eased. "You won't scream?"

She shook her head, realizing the wisdom of this filthy little trooper's warning.

The hand moved away.

The face didn't.

She felt the first of a series of tremblings ripple through her, and her eyes filled with tears.

"You're gonna be okay," the soldier said kindly. "It's safe here."

The tank fired again.

"How . . . how can you tell?"

He jerked a knowing thumb over his shoulder. "If we don't stop it here, I got this gut feeling it's gonna head on into town. I ain't never seen anything look so pissed in my life."

Contrary to her distressed feelings of a moment before, Phyllis grabbed for his soiled and somewhat hairy hand and pulled it to her modest bosom. "You won't leave me here all alone, will you? Please say you won't."

He shifted until he could sit beside her. "Gonna have to, lady. Those are my buddies down there. I can't leave them to fight alone." He glanced around quickly and expertly. "You got good cover here. You got your night. I don't think it'll find you, *if* it comes back, which I don't think it will come back." His gaze moved to the angle of the slope and followed it as far as he could in the dark. "Damn, that must've been one mother of a ship."

"Demons," she said primly, "do not travel in ships."

"This one did, lady."

He extricated his hand and proceeded to fashion a serviceable lean-to out of birch bark, pinecones, and mountain laurel branches. She watched the construction in amazement, saying nothing, shuddering and only whimpering each time the tank's cannon fired, each time the monster that had taken her darling from her bellowed in response.

Then, before she knew it, she was inside, huddled on a bed of leaves.

The unsavory little corporal grinned at her. "Stick it out for a while before you cut out," he advised. "No shit, no bear's gonna come around while that thing's still in the neighborhood."

"You sure you have to go?"

"Yeah. You know how it is."

She reached out and touched the back of his hand, proud that her skin only crawled a little. "God be with you, Corporal."

"Thanks."

"And . . . and thank you for saving my life."

"Hey, I'm that kinda guy, y'know?"

And he was gone, out of her life as quickly as he had crawled into it.

The fighting continued.

And Phyllis, alone and helpless in the infernal light of battle, said, "Bears? What bears?"

Officer Lucian Twiller staggered out of the woods, his braid askew, his cap long since vanished, his right ankle throbbing, the knees of his pants shredded, the buttons of his uniform tunic popped and gone, his shoes maddeningly scuffed, his service revolver snug in his hand.

Smith was going to pay for this, the righteous little bastard. No one sets Lucian Twiller up for an ambush, then leaves him alone to die in the wilderness. No one.

He looked up when a shadow blotted out the stars.

His mouth fell agape.

Was that a convoluted horn he saw before him, sweeping down out of the shadow toward the musculature of his chest?

"Oh boy," he said, automatically emptying his gun into the shadow's groin.

And IT said in crooning anger, "Lucy, you got some esplainin' to do!"

Master Sergeant Porter Wagoneer, after seeing that dumb little prick Delphim ride off with the major in the Jeep, rallied his bedeviled and bedraggled forces into a modest clump behind the tank.

Nothing had worked.

Neither the cannon nor the rocket launchers nor the bullets nor three or four bayonets had been able to put a dent in the monster that had turned his life into a living Hell, a waking nightmare, a solid mirage of death and destruction.

But it wasn't his duty to wonder why he, of all the dogfaces in all the armies in all the world, had been chosen to be the first to make contact with a creature from outer space. That's just the way it was in this man's army, and as long as he did his duty, and did it well, his ass was covered when the court-martial team wanted to know how in hell he'd managed to lose nearly a hundred men with the most sophisticated ground weaponry in the world to a *Thing* that had only a few claws, a few teeth, a horn or two, a ray beam, a ton or so of muscle in every limb, and a penchant for quoting Buffalo Bob each time it squashed a private.

The tank rumbled forward.

The sergeant, his arms leaden and his shoulders aching from fire and recoil, dispatched a small group into the trees, with orders to work their way around the *Thing*, in hopes of finding an Achilles' heel.

It might have worked.

He might have been a hero.

But at that moment, someone said, "Hey, Sarge!" and he saw Milos Athnos break out of the trees, slide down the short

but steep embankment into the ditch, and scream when the
Thing whirled around and saw him.

"No!" Wagoneer yelled.

"Sarge!" a buck private shouted.

Wagoneer didn't hear him. It was too much. It was all too
much, and no fucking dirtball from no fucking foreign planet
was going to grind his best buddy into the ground and live to
tell about it. Not as long as Master Sergeant Porter Wagoneer
was around.

With a grenade in one hand and an M-60 machine gun in
the other, he charged around the side of the tank.

His men screamed at him.

The *Thing* whirled back and snarled.

Athnos, scrambling back up the bank on his back, saw him
and desperately tried to wave him to the safety of the tank.

The sergeant would have none of it.

This was his show now.

On the dead run, which image he wished he hadn't thought
of under the circumstances, he heaved one grenade at its belly,
threw himself out of the way of what might have been a four-
clawed paw, rolled between three or four legs, he couldn't
tell, and came up firing the M-60 into the juncture of whatever the hell the goddamned *Thing* used to stand on. At the
same time, he dug another grenade from his pocket, let the
pin go, counted, then lobbed it at what he thought was a
spiked tail as he rolled again out of the way, still firing, dig-
ging into another pocket for yet another grenade.

Athnos begged him to get away while he could.

Wagoneer only laughed, threw the grenade at one eye or
another, rolled away still firing, and came up at the edge of
the ditch.

"Milos," he called over his shoulder, "are you all right?"

"Shit no, I'm gonna die!"

Wagoneer laughed at his friend's enormous courage in the
face of the face—if it was a face—of the *Thing* that now faced
him.

He laughed so hard, he didn't see the paw, or the claw, or
the stinger, or the triangular scale, slice down through the
murky air and through the hard rind of his stomach.

He felt it, though.

And the force of the blow lifted him off his feet and carried him backward, into his buddy's lap.

The *Thing* turned its attention back to the tank, which had made a clever end run around it and sped off toward Gander Pond.

"Aw shit," the sergeant groaned as the pain finally hit him.

"You got it bad, buddy," Athnos said, his voice choked with emotion.

"Yeah, I know." He gritted his teeth. "Shit. Shit. Shit!"

The corporal tried to ease up the embankment again, this time hauling his friend and mentor after him. But Wagoneer screamed and shook his head.

"No good, pal," the sergeant said, hissing with agony. "Lordy Jesus, that smarts."

The monster lumbered after the tank.

"Medic!" Athnos cried.

The remaining troopers scattered as if on command—some into the forest, some after the alien though not quite as fast, some back toward the roadblock where several other Jeeps had been left in the care of two privates who only had to shave every second Tuesday.

After a moment, Wagoneer shifted slightly. "Getting dark, old buddy."

Athnos nodded. "Yeah. Gets that way after midnight out here in the boonies."

The sergeant laughed, coughed, spat blood, and sighed. "Y'know, I remember that time in Manila."

"Yeah."

"What a bitch."

"Yeah. Take it easy, Port. We'll get you taken care of, no sweat, just take it slow." Athnos raised his head and his voice. "Medic, goddamnit!"

Wagoneer reached up a hand and grabbed his friend's shirt. "Too late, you dumb Greek, too late. Guess I rocked when I should've rolled."

"You always were stupid without me, you fathead."

"Yeah."

"Yeah."

Time passed.

All the flares finally died.

"Milos?"

"Still here."

"Got a confession to make."

"Hey, man, you don't gotta spill your guts to me."

Wagoneer shrugged. "Gotta say it, though."

The corporal gripped his friend's hand. Hard.

"You know that little lady you was seeing, back down Georgia, when we was thinking about getting out?"

"Yeah. Yeah, I remember. Redhead."

"That's her."

"What about her?"

A bat darted across the road.

They heard the cannon fire, far away.

"I porked her when you were on leave."

Athnos chuckled. "I know."

Wagoneer opened his eyes. "You know?"

"Sure. I wasn't on leave. I was porking your wife."

"No shit. Which one?"

He never heard the answer. Pain rode on spasms through his system, instantly shutting everything down but his eyes. He looked up at the fading stars, saw the dim face of the moon, saw the tops of the trees, saw Athnos smiling down at him, a hint of light in one eye.

"Hey, Greek," he gasped.

The corporal leaned over.

"That really is one ugly sonofabitch."

He coughed.

He slumped.

Corporal Milos Athnos vowed revenge.

"God damn," Horace O'Malley muttered as he picked his way clumsily through the windblown destruction of his newspaper's spacious reception room. Twice already he had barked his shins in the dark, twice he had collided with a wall that shouldn't have been there, and three times he had fallen over the debris scattered over the sawdust-covered floor.

Finally, however, he made it to his back office, fell into his swivel chair, and grabbed up the telephone.

He crossed his fingers.

The dial tone hummed at him.

He thanked the Lord for such a wondrous blessing and

promised never again to call Phyllis Lager for meditations
when her husband was out of town, saving souls at funeral
director conventions.

A fire engine hooted outside.

He dialed a number, waited impatiently, then said, "William, this is Horace. Do not interrupt me. Do not ask me
questions. Just get your little network ass out here as fast as
you can. I think you're gonna want to see what's happening
in your old hometown."

He listened.

He held up the receiver as another fire engine screamed
past.

"You hear that, boy? That's for real. We ain't having a
goddamn party out here, and Long Island Smith ain't gotten
into the liquor store again. Whole lot of shit is going down,
army's sneaking around, planes are crashing like flies on the
mountain, and I'm putting out a special edition tomorrow
morning."

He listened.

"Shit, man, for all I know the Cubans have landed. Just
get out here, and make sure you pronounce my name right."

He slammed the receiver down, picked it up, dialed another number, and scowled when his daughter, Kitty, didn't
answer the home phone. He hoped she was all right, and
knew she would understand that this was her father's last
chance to make a name for himself. A good girl, she was.
Just like her mother, God rest her soul. He only wished he
were able to spend more quality time with her. Whatever the
hell that meant.

Oh well. He dialed a third number.

"Darlin', this is Horace. You ever want to yell 'Stop the
presses'?"

He listened.

"Then yell it now, honey, 'cause I got a story that'll win
us both a Pulitzer."

He listened.

He grinned.

He said, "Would you believe a mountain that burns with
purple fire?"

A scowl when he heard someone crashing around in the
front. A roll of his eyes, half rising from his chair, and he

said, "Darlin', I ain't got time to argue with you. I just talked to William, he's sending out a crew by helicopter. If you want to—"

A shadow stood in the office doorway.

"Hold it a second, darlin'," he said, and cupped a hand over the mouthpiece. "Kitty, that you?"

A derisive snort for an answer.

"Then who the hell are you, and what the hell are you doing in my office?"

A rock-hard feminine voice answered, "Mr. O'Malley, I am a representative of the Armed Forces of the United States of America. And if you don't put that phone down, right now, I'm going to blow your brains out."

·3·

The moment the creature became sort of visible on the highway, and as soon as Kent pointed out its appearance to Chita, she shrieked and darted into the Gander Palace, screaming at him to move it or lose it, because she wasn't about to stick around, in the open, when she knew that the whore with the scientist had a private arsenal they could use to defend themselves against interplanetary aggression.

By the time she had finished, Kent was breathless. And immobile.

"Kent!" she called.

Very well, he thought, squared both chin and shoulders, and managed not to flinch when the tank took out a good portion of the road a good hundred yards shy of the monster lumbering toward town.

"Kent!"

He noted again the blank space where the guard's desk had been, then ducked through the fire door and took the stairs two at a time to the fifth floor, one at a time after that, and finally caught up with her on the top floor.

She wasn't panting.

"Why aren't you panting?" he asked.

"I took the elevator," she answered. "Why? Did you take the stairs?"

He smiled tightly. "I had to see if anyone needed my assistance."

She grinned.

Casopia called to them from an open bronze and walnut
door, which opened onto a gold-and-silver-flocked foyer,
which in turn led to nine main rooms, each with extensive
views on all sides, expensive Victorian reproduction furni-
ture, dignified artwork, and carpets thick enough to lose a
dog team in.

Everything was either red or white.

Except for the kitchen, which was empty.

"In here," she said, ushering them into a large airy room
whose floor-to-ceiling walls were tinted glass. There were no
chairs, only dozens of thick, fringed pillows, none less than
four feet on a side, all of them scattered across the floor in
such a way that walking was much like a wobbly balancing
act. She stood at the east wall, overlooking Gander Mountain.
They ranged themselves behind her and watched with increasing dismay the rebirth of the flares' aerial display, the
ground display of flaring rifles and bazookas, and the parking
lot display of the horn player trying to get his mouth around
the top of Kent's Dilemma.

The alien's form was once again obscured by all the smoke.

But it was there.

A broadside ray to the Palace's private garage proved that;
it also proved how combustible ludicrously expensive automobiles could be.

Casopia shuddered. "I think they and it are getting closer."

Kent knew that.

"I suggest we save what we can and get the hell out of
here."

Kent had thought of that.

"And what about my dream?" Hooker asked her petu-
lantly.

Kent didn't remember it.

"Aliens?" She covered her mouth and giggled.

Kent remembered.

"If it's true," the man insisted heatedly, "we cannot shirk
our duty as intelligent members of the predominant race of
this planet. We must try to contact it. Or them."

Kent didn't think it wise.

"You're crazy," Chita snapped.

Good point, Kent thought.

"Why? Because I happen to have a dream?" Hooker said

angrily, his fists and teeth clenched. "Because I don't automatically charge into savage battle against the unknown simply because it is the unknown? Because I am not afraid of the dark? Because I dare to think where no man has thought before?"

Kent glanced around the room. Another good point.

"I admire you, Nick," Casopia sighed with batting eyelids. "Honestly I do. But quite frankly, after what happened to Tobacco Joe out there, I vote for not dying."

Got it in one, Kent agreed.

Hooker glared at them, his face flushed with rage. His mouth opened, closed, and he stomped across the pillows and out of the room. Some moments later, a door slammed.

Casopia paled. "Oh my."

A volley of gunfire rattled the walls.

Hooker returned and stumbled to Casopia's side. "Your bathroom," he said, "is all mirrors."

She winked. "Kind of cute, huh?"

Kent considered the possibilities from all angles and decided that, all in all, he'd rather remain in the dark.

"This," Chita said in disgust, "is getting us nowhere. Don't you people have any balls?"

Casopia looked bemused.

"May I say something?" Kent offered as the room brightened as if lightning had struck nearby.

An explosion.

A horn blaring as if it were stuck.

The building trembled.

The red ray swept across the sky and topped four acres of old oak and hulking sycamore.

They waited.

Kent pointed to the night. "As much as I admire Dr. Hooker's dream, and certainly feel a certain kinship with that alien out there—*if* it is an alien, that is, and we've as yet no solid proof of that except that we've never seen anything quite like it before on this planet—I should like to point out that both our flight from this beleaguered valley and our desire to gain knowledge from a possible traveler from the stars are rather beside the point."

He clasped his hands behind his back.

"Out there," he continued, pointing as best he could with

a shoulder, "there is a war going on. I would suspect that the military has blocked all roads, closed all airports, and shut down all train stations. Which leaves us with, as I see it, only two alternatives."

He paused dramatically.

Another explosion.

The horn stopped blaring.

"First," he said, "we accede to Dr. Hooker's demand that we attempt to contact this thing and discover what it wants. We may learn a great deal. We may come away with several secrets of the universe. We may even discover that all it wants is peace and harmony between our species."

"Bravo," said the scientist. "Good man."

"Tell that to the headless horseman," Chita muttered.

"Or secondly," Kent went on, ignoring them both and the way Casopia kept taking deep breaths to calm herself down, "we must either prepare to defend ourselves right here against hostile incursion or repair to town, where we must do our best to aid our friends and neighbors in the protection of the community which has nurtured us all these years.

"In either case, we shall need some personal protection of our own."

He smiled.

They waited.

He sniffed and rocked on his heels.

Chita said, "Is that it?"

"It is," he said.

"Where's the part about hiding in the woods?"

He frowned. "What part about hiding in the woods?"

"The part that says we scrounge up stuff to eat, something to drink, grab some of these pillow things, and hide out in the woods until this is all over. That part."

He looked down at her in disappointment. "Chita, what about that speech you just gave me, out in the parking lot?"

She shrugged. "Hey, I'm a working girl, Lord. I got my priorities, y'know?"

He sighed.

They waited.

Kent gave them his best *make up your minds before the building falls down* look.

Hooker looked at Casopia, touched her shoulder tenderly,

and said, "I suppose . . . it might be possible . . . if one doesn't work . . . we just might . . ."

"You're being very elliptical, Doctor," Kent scolded mildly.

"Hell," Chita said, "let's just blow the sonofabitch up and get back to my party."

Hooker frowned. "Party?"

"An expression," the waitress explained. "It's American."

"Ah."

The building trembled again; there was no explosion.

"I fear I fear the worst, my friends," Kent said, tripping to the east wall and placing his hands on the fragile glass.

"In that case," Casopia said with determined jutting jaw, and a grab for Hooker's arm, "since we don't have much choice, you might as well follow me."

"About time," Chita told her. "I thought you were going to yak all night."

Kent listened to them leave, heard a door open, heard Chita exclaim in high-pitched delight and Hooker moan in either despair or ecstasy. He had no idea what the curious woman on the tenth floor of the Gander Palace had shown them, but he knew he wouldn't like it.

A glance out the window. The musical trio had pried the horn player off the Dilemma and was even now, as he watched, burning rubber toward town in a perfectly preserved '34 yellow Cord, the old woman driving, the pair of old men cringing in the back.

Good luck, my unknown friends, he saluted. Good luck and God speed.

"Yo, Lord!" Chita called from the doorway.

"Holy Toledo!" exclaimed Ham Delphim.

He stood in the office of the Gander Pond newspaper and bit his lips to keep his mouth from falling open.

The major was at the desk, behind which sat a rather undistinguished, decidedly overweight editor.

The major had taken off the regulation combat helmet and shaken out the most beautiful, shoulder-length black hair he had ever seen in his life.

Jeez, he thought, Major Settbach is a woman!

"Now look here, Major," O'Malley sputtered indignantly, "you can't just walk into a free American news office and take over without a judge, a lawyer, and four hundred different kinds of writs that suspend my constitutional rights under the Fourth Amendment."

"Fifth," said Major Wendy Settbach.

"Whatever the hell."

"Private," the major said.

"Yessir! Ma'am! Sir!" He shrugged weakly.

"Shoot this man in the knee if he so much as spits toward that telephone."

"Major?"

"Damnit, Major!"

Major Settbach drew her .45 and smiled. "Mr. O'Malley, in case you hadn't noticed, we are currently under siege by a force which none of us yet can even pretend to understand. We do not have time for all the niceties you civilians so blithely take for granted." In thoughtful warning, she rubbed the barrel of the gun against her cheek. "Take my word for it—you *will* be shot if you disobey my orders."

"But why the phone?" O'Malley demanded.

"Because if word of this gets out," she explained wearily, "if we do not use all the manpower and weaponry we have at hand to contain this vile thing which you don't yet know about but will in a very few minutes, there will be such a panic in this world that God only knows how many will die as a result, God only knows what forces will be unleashed to kill thousands more, and God sure as hell is the only one who knows why we, Mr. Free Press O'Malley, *have been invaded by Mars*."

The editor looked at the private, who grinned and patted his rifle.

The major looked at the editor, who sank back into his chair and said, "Major, I have a godawful feeling that I am now covered by all the shit that hit the fan a few seconds before you walked in."

"You made a call," said Settbach flatly.

O'Malley held up two fingers.

"Well, hell." She plopped onto the corner of the desk, scratched her temple with her gun, and looked at the ceiling.

"You know, there are days when nothing in the whole god-damn world goes right. You know?"

"I do," O'Malley said.

"I'll bet," the major muttered, pushed herself off the desk, and marched to the door. "Private, that order still stands. I've got some defenses to work out."

"Now wait a minute, Major!" O'Malley protested.

A tank rumbled past the office, its still smoking cannon facing rearward.

"Don't think we have a minute," the major said with a sour grin. "Looks like that shit of yours just came down from the ceiling."

O'Malley leapt to his feet and banged a fist on the desk. "But what about reinforcements? Surely you don't think a town like this, even with your men, can hold off whatever it is you're running from."

Major Settbach smiled sweetly over her shoulder. "Mr. O'Malley, I am a major because I am good at what I do. And what I do is think ahead."

A supremely dejected Mayor James Ellader scurried away from the newspaper office, hoping that the major hadn't seen him skulking around, eavesdropping, and discovering that his plans to put Gander Pond squarely on the map via the good auspices of the information media were now shot all to hell and gone.

Cut off from the outside world indeed!

Nuts.

If he didn't think of something to counter this development, and think of it soon, there might not be anything left of his town to put on the map.

A puzzle.

He would have to do some quick, serious thinking here if this entire affair wasn't going to turn out to be a disaster. It was his duty. It was his obligation. It was why the folks had voted him into office twice.

Unfortunately a mayor was only as good as his last picture in a tri-state newspaper or his last interview on a New York news station. Lately things had been, admittedly, a little on the dry side.

It wasn't as if he wasn't a good mayor. Even his wife had

told him several times that he had had his moments. But a *great* mayor would be able to turn adversity into gainful publicity at the drop of a hat.

James Ellader wanted desperately to be a great mayor.

"James?"

Startled, he looked up and saw his wife on the corner. Cheeks flushed, eyes watery, she seemed ready to begin one of her weep sessions, right here in public. Even as he approached her with exaggerated sympathy lest anyone be watching while tending to their wounds, he groaned silently. Eunice's problem was, she was always weeping. The damned dog craps on the carpet, she weeps; the cable television drops her favorite channel, she weeps; he gets elected for his second four-year term, she weeps.

"Yes, darling," he said, barely containing his impatience.

"It's Uncle Bill."

Of course. Why not? It's always Uncle Bill. King of the freeloaders, master of the snide, collector of more Danish pornography than any right-thinking American ought to have.

"Yes, darling?"

Maybe the old guy croaked.

A fire truck screamed by, lights and sirens and firemen and not a single damned reporter within camera distance.

Eunice dabbed at her eyes with a handkerchief. "He's dead."

James looked heavenward and raised an eyebrow.

"The explosion . . . his heart . . . I don't know what to do . . . funeral arrangements . . . flowers—"

He took her arm tenderly. "Eunice, we're in the middle of an invasion here. I don't think we'll have to worry about funeral stuff for a while."

She wept.

"Where is he?"

"They took him to the funeral parlor."

"I see." He feigned a thoughtful frown while rubbing his chin and tapping his foot. Suddenly he blinked and realized where they were. "Darling," he said, turning her around with practiced ease and haste, "perhaps, during this time of stress, you might want to sit with him."

"Do you think so?"

"Of course. He was your favorite uncle, remember? He would have wanted it that way."

A sobbing sigh. "I suppose so. And it will help keep my mind off this disaster business."

He nodded. He smiled. He walked with her part of the way to be sure she wouldn't change her mind. And as soon as she had regained control, her expression molded into that *I'm in charge again* look he'd first seen on their honeymoon, he raced back to the corner and grinned at the mass of broken glass on the sidewalk, the disrupted display inside, and all that lovely equipment just sitting there.

Waiting for him.

And media destiny.

Artie Chong had never met a woman like that in his entire life, except for his darling panda of the pampas, Sophia. There she'd been, in full military regalia, riding by in that Jeep driven by a kid whose ears stuck out wider than radar dishes, when she saw him on the side of the road, trying to get that stupid horse away from an overturned pickup filled with hay.

She'd talked with the horse.

She'd talked with him.

And now, here he was, riding with the wind toward a secret outpost deep in the Kittatinny Mountains.

"To save the world," she had breathed into his hot little ear.

He only hoped she could save his little tinted ass when his wife found out.

Kent Montana, who really didn't give a damn about his real name anymore and hoped his mother had been caught in a storm somewhere off the coast of Majorca so that he could be an orphan except for his sister, decided that he should have committed suicide when he had the chance.

It would have been, all in all, the honorable thing.

"What," he said to Chita, "is that thing?"

She opened her mouth.

He held up a hand. "Never mind."

On any other day, in any other place, he wouldn't have minded standing in a room full of fringed pillows, facing a woman who looked as if she had just fallen into an armory

and come up smelling like cordite; ordinarily he might have
thought that the machine gun she had braced so chicly against
her hip was, for her, more than somehow appropriate; on a
good day, he might even have entertained the possibility that
the loaded ammo belts she had draped over her shoulders and
chest were some sort of wartime fashion statement.

But this was ridiculous.

"You like it?" she said gleefully.

"It's you," he answered glumly.

She beckoned with the barrel. "C'mon, Lord—"

"Baron."

"—we got something for you too."

She disappeared into the hallway.

He looked behind him at the star flares and the *Thing* that
walked beneath them.

He heard Nicodemus exclaiming over what could not have
been the latest in armor-piercing shells.

As he sighed and hastened toward the rear of the condominium, he thought he heard Casopia explaining how to load
said armor-piercing shells into something that all the scientist
had to do was brace against his shoulder, aim, and fire, as
long as no one stood behind him.

The hallway was long, the only open door at the far end.
Chita stood at the threshold, grinning, then standing aside
when he reached her.

"This," she said, "you ain't going to believe."

He believed it.

He believed it because he was here and he was awake; he
believed it because if he believed that aliens had landed on
Earth he had no choice; and he believed it because as soon
as he stepped into the room, Casopia thrust an M-16 into his
hands and said, "Give a butler this sucker and no one, but
no one, is going to be late for dinner."

He tried to find the words to ask her where she had gotten
all the handguns he saw in open hope chests lined up against
the walls; he sputtered as he attempted to learn where she
had managed to find all the rifles, hand machine guns, and
what looked like rocket launchers bracketed on those walls;
he couldn't even begin to formulate the questions that would
inform him where in God's name she had gotten the hunting

bows, the crossbows, the pikes, the two lances, and the harbor mine.

The woman smiled. "A little overwhelming, isn't it?"

He nodded.

"Something I fell into a few years ago," she said, "when a general and I got a little rank." She grinned. "Keeps the wolves from the door."

No shit, he thought.

Hooker hefted the bazooka he'd been caressing and said, "If I weren't such a pacifist, I'd be having an orgasm."

Chita set her weapon down butt-first and leaned on it. "So. You think we got enough here to take care of what's out there?"

He found his voice at last, cowering somewhere in the vicinity of his loins. "To take Fort Knox, perhaps. I'm not sure about what's out there."

"Well, why not?" she demanded.

"The army doesn't seem to be doing such a hot job, does it?"

She gave the army a prolonged raspberry. "You see those guys before? They can't even storm a weatherman, for god's sake." She tapped the butt with her finger. "I think we call ourselves The Lord's Avengers."

He almost laughed. "That sounds like a church group." A glance around the room, an internal sigh, and he added as the walls trembled and a crossbow fell to the floor, "We'd best not be here much longer."

They agreed.

They chose backpacks from the wilderness collection in another room and filled them with ammunition and smaller sundries; they checked the kitchen for food—"Don't be silly. I eat out"—and wasted no time rushing back down the stairs to the lobby.

"We'll use the cars," Kent told them. "Both, in case one of us doesn't make it."

"Me and you," Chita said with a nod.

"And we must hurry. If that creature gets ahead of us, I don't how we'll make it."

They hurried.

With Chita riding shotgun, he fired up the Dilemma and screeched out of the parking lot, was nearly sideswiped by two soldier-filled Jeeps as he hit the highway, and followed them onto the road into Gander Pond.

He could not see Hooker in the rearview mirror.

"It's all right," Chita said when she noticed his concern. "They can take care of themselves."

"I know."

"So don't worry."

"I'm not worried about them."

"So what are you worried about?"

"It's hard to explain," he said.

She nodded her understanding. "Try anyway. I always find it's better to talk these things out."

"What things?"

"The things that trouble you."

"But I don't know."

"You just said you did."

"Ah." He nodded. "What I meant was, I know what's troubling me, but I don't know what, if anything, the trouble is."

"Ah," she said. "So what's the trouble?"

"Gander Pond."

"Yes."

"I hope it's all right."

"Hey," she said, slapping his knee, "don't worry, Baron. It's all right, okay? We get there, we save them, we go away for a while and write our autobiographies. We got a little trouble here, but what the hell, right?"

"Right."

Wrong, he thought. The woman was a maniac. And she still hadn't answered his question—how his adopted temporary home was holding up under all this alien pressure.

As he swerved around the wreckage of a pickup, he trusted it was in better shape than Gander Pond.

· 4 ·

Gander Pond was in serious trouble.

· 4a ·

It was horrible.

–III–

Special Effects

✦ 1 ✦

"Now listen up, people!"

Above the rooftops of Gander Pond, the eastern horizon glowed angrily, its hellish light pulsing like a metropolitan borealis gone mad. Bathed in such crimson and gold misery, the surrounding hills seemed to shimmer and shift, advance and retreat, making all who watched the display disoriented and disturbed; the stars were washed out when the light intensified, and when the light subsided, the waning moon seemed stained a solemn red. Eyes watered and nostrils flared in discomfort whenever the summer wind shifted and wafted the smoke and its attendant stench of battle over the town.

And through it all, the horrific tympanic beat of intermittent explosions, booming and crashing, accompanied by the fearsome bellowing of an unearthly creature.

"Hey, listen up!"

At street level, the cleanup process had been aborted when the tank and Jeeps filled with weary soldiers rumbled into town and took up a defensive posture—the tank straddling the white line with cannon aimed east, the Jeeps parked diagonally from curb to curb, their battle-hardened passengers crouched expectantly behind them. Thus were there shards of glass glittering still in the gutters, tattered napkins and scraps of paper fluttering helplessly through the air, and bits of singed clothing and people still stuck to crumbling walls, bent streetlamps, and the rusted teeth of empty storm drains.

Here and there houses still burned; eventually the movie

theater roof collapsed; the mortuary's basement was reasonably instantly flooded when a minor water pipe burst; and Eunice Ellader spent a good hour chasing what was left of her Uncle Bill down Elm Street toward the circus.

It was a nightmare.

A few of the critically injured were still tended to by Good Samaritans plaintively crying out for medics and ambulances. Those who were able to walk did so, as quickly as possible, west. The four hotels, finally able to run on the strength of their own private generators, generously opened their lobbies and bars to the emotionally battered and afflicted for nominal charges; the restaurants created soup-and-salad kitchens for those unable to make their way home; and the police department steadfastly maintained its presence wherever possible in order to stave off panic and make sure that all who were in need of assistance were able to find it.

"Hey, I'm talking to you!"

The whole situation was barely three inches shy of complete chaos.

Even Private First Class Ham Delphim's untrained eye could see that, which was why he could not understand why none of the civilians paid any attention to Major Settbach, standing so nobly and inspirationally atop the tank and trying to get people to pay attention to her. It was incredible. She was, after all, the U.S. Army. She also had the tank. And no one else seemed willing to assume the leadership position. To his mind, it was crime. Like that hotshot newspaper editor, who had thought the major was bluffing about the telephone call. As soon as she left the office, the man had given Ham a man-to-man wink and reached for the receiver.

Ham shot it out of his hand.

The editor blanched.

Ham yanked the wire from the wall, saluted, and made his way to the street, where, after a second's confusion, he saw the well-turned soldierly figure of his very own major standing alongside the tank's cannon, one hand on her hip, the other on her .45. The sight had nearly brought him to tears.

"Damnit, you scum for brains, this is an order! Listen the hell up!"

No one on the street even turned a head.

And when her fifth demand for rightful recognition went

unheeded, he wondered what Sergeant Wagoneer would do in a situation like this.

He blinked rapidly. The very thought of his late mentor brought bitter tears to his eyes. Fabian Lamanza had told the story dozens of times, and even now, Ham could not help but feel a lump in his throat, a weight in his stomach, a surge of rage that added years to his young, innocent face.

What *would* the sergeant do?

"Jesus H., people, you got a death wish or something! Pay attention here! I got a tank! I got troops! My God!"

Three minutes later he figured it out.

With a decisive, no-turning-back-now adjustment of his combat helmet, he marched smartly to the front of the tank, slapped in a fresh clip of ammunition, set his M-16 on automatic, and fired into the sky.

Immediately everyone quieted.

No one moved.

There was nothing but the mournful cry of the wind, and the far-off sound of the *Thing* blowing something up.

"Thank you, Private," the major said.

Private Ham Delphim only nodded grimly. He was a man now; there was no need for public displays of emotion. The sarge, he thought, would have been proud.

With a long tolerant sigh, Sophia Chong stared at the worn broom in her hand, measured its firepower against the head of Mayor James Ellader, and considered the rewards of ritual execution. In times of crisis, there couldn't possibly be any drawbacks.

And crisis this was.

The Pagoda, despite the heroic work of the patrons left standing after the purple explosion, was damn near a complete loss. Most of the ceiling was down in the planters, two of the walls were cracked through, and the kitchen spouted more steam than Artie after he'd had a few sips of her homemade wine. She had even given up trying to clear the pavement, so depressed was her current mood.

Ellader hadn't helped.

"The point is," he explained for the third time, a wary gaze on the broom, one hand tucked behind his back, "that you are a leading member of this community and not without some influence. You must therefore understand that this disaster has made a mess of our summer. It will take us years to recover, financially speaking.''

She leaned on the broomstick and nodded toward the tank and the Jeeps and the red-face shouting major. "How about physically, huh? You think financially is bad, how about the job of rebuilding all the stuff that fell down? Not to mention the holes in the road, the movie theater, the water system under the mortuary, and—''

Ellader smiled at her.

Sophia was reminded of a Warner Brothers shark.

The mayor brought his hidden hand out. In it was a compact videotape camera with power zoom lens and omnidirectional microphone.

"My hair's a mess,'' she protested automatically.

A fire engine shrieked by. Ellader immediately brought the viewfinder to his eyes and followed the vehicle's bumpy progress around the tank. "We just haven't got the funds, Sophia,'' he said, panning along the street. "You know that as well as I do. Federal and state disaster money will take forever to get here, and won't be enough even when it does. Insurance companies won't touch us with a ten-foot pole unless we take them to court.'' He lowered the camera. "It took me a while, but the way I see it, TV-movie revenues is the only way we can swing it and be back in business by next year.''

"You're an idiot.''

Dropping down on one knee, he taped what was left of the front of the Pagoda.

"Look, all we got to do is write a script around these pictures and we can have this sucker on the air in less than a month.'' He looked up at her. "That's after we sell selected bits to the newspeople.''

Oh, Artie, she thought, where are you when I need you?

Ellader's voice dropped to a conspiratorial whisper as he straightened. "Besides, we're going to be famous, right? We'll all be in it, Sophia, all of us. They aren't even going to have to hire actors.''

She glared at him. "Wonderful. And what about the human suffering, huh? What about the injured, the dying, the blood, the loss of limb and flesh?''

He tapped a cassette poking out of his jacket pocket. "Got it all right here."

The broom moved of its own volition. She was sure of it. One minute it was pressed against the sidewalk, the next it was pressed against the side of the mayor's head. Which slammed into the videotape camera. Which slammed into a portion of the Pagoda which, until now, had remained unscathed.

The wall held.

The camera didn't.

Ellader jumped back and stared at the ruins of his equipment. "Well, damn," he said. He whirled, his expression enraged, his eyes filling with angry tears. "Damnit, Sophia, why'd you do that?"

"Because," she explained.

He shook his head morosely. "I'll never get it done now. Shit. Nuts." He spread his hands pathetically. "Sophia, we could've been something, you know? We could've been big, real big. We could've been known all over the world! We could've been somebody!"

A distant explosion made them look east.

"I think," she told him, "we already are."

They exchanged knowing glances.

Sophia dropped the broom.

The mayor whispered, "I wonder if O'Malley has one of these things."

Then someone fired a rifle into the air and the street fell silent.

Horace O'Malley sat at his desk for nearly ten minutes after the army left him, listening to the sound effects of battle in the distance, listening to that bitch of a major trying to restore order in the streets, and staring at the mess that jug-eared private had made of his telephone.

It wasn't fair.

It just wasn't fair.

The biggest story of his professional life, of the entire life of the entire damned planet, and it looked as if he was going to have to do all the goddamn work himself if he was going to get any credit at all at the end of this mess.

As he rooted through his desk for a pen and pad, he ruminated on the sad state of press treatment these days, and on the deterioration of respect for the ass-busting editors who made sure that the public's right to know was placed in their hands every morning before breakfast. And when his ruminations were over, he hoisted himself off his seat and tripped and stumbled his way to the sidewalk.

The major was on the tank.

Several Jeeps were parked up the road, forming a barrier between Main Street and the way out of town.

Two dozen or so soldiers in full battle gear were crouched behind both tank and Jeeps, weapons at the ready. He could see a few of them hastily scribbling letters to, no doubt, their mothers and sweethearts.

The major shouted something.

O'Malley ignored it—he could always ask her what she said, later, after she cleaned it up—and hurried over to the nearest trooper, who was stationed behind a lamppost, grenade in one hand, grenade launcher in the other. Hell, he thought; Kitty should be doing this stuff, not me. What the hell's a newspaperman's daughter for anyway, if not to feed her old man the innards of history? Hell.

A deep breath then, and hoping he hadn't lost the touch, and O'Malley tapped the trooper on the shoulder and flashed his yellowed press card. "Son," he said solemnly, "how do you feel, knowing that the world as we know it just may be coming to an end and you'll probably die before dawn?"

The soldier stared at him.

O'Malley, editorially wise in the ways of eliciting facts and innuendo, smiled and handed him a cigarette. The young man nodded his thanks, lit it with one hand, and blew sardonic smoke toward the edge of town.

"Can't think about things like that, sir," he said at last. "Gotta do my duty."

"Of course you do, son. But aren't you worried about your family?"

"Ain't got one. I'm an orphan. All I got's my rifle and my bunk."

O'Malley nodded, jotted the response on his pad, and duck-walked to an older man kneeling at the back bumper of a mud-splattered Jeep. He introduced himself, and the soldier gave him a gap-toothed smile.

"Son," the editor said, "how does it feel, knowing that you're soon going to probably die for your country at the hands or whatever of some raging interstellar beast?"

An explosion cast an orange light over the scene, and the echoes off the hills seemed to last forever.

"Well," the soldier replied, accurately spitting tobacco juice disdainfully in the direction of the explosion, "seems t'me we got two choices, you know what I mean? I mean, we either give in to them godless Commie bastards or we fight them to our doorsteps. Ain't no fun living in a country where they tell you when to shit, if you know what I mean."

O'Malley tapped his pad thoughtfully. "But we're not fighting Communists," he corrected politely. "It's a monster from outer space."

"Yeah, well, it's from Mars, right?"

"Right."

"Mars is the Red Planet, right?"

"Sure."

"Well, then, there you go."

After some considerable thought, he jotted the response on his pad and moved down to the next man in line, who was large in both girth and height, wearing a flak jacket, combat helmet obscured by lots of leafy twigs, and facial camouflage.

The major shouted.

A window shattered.

"Outta my face," the soldier growled as the editor framed his next question.

"Now wait a minute," O'Malley protested.

The soldier grabbed his pen and ate it. "Outta my face, boy, or I start looking for dessert."

The editor considered standing on his rights as a reporter and demanding that the man tell him his innermost thoughts, then stood on his feet and moved to the next trooper, who took his cue from the third man and ate the pad. O'Malley nearly wept. How the hell was he supposed to remember all this? What had happened to the public's right to know? Where had it all gone, the fedoras and the Smith-Coronas and the bourbon in the bar after a hard day's scavenging?

Where the hell was Clark Kent when you needed him?

Where the hell was Kitty?

Someone fired a rifle not five feet from where he stood,

and O'Malley decided that before he sucked up to the major, he'd best first change his pants.

On the far side of the street, seated on the curb with a cigarette dangling languidly between his lips, his black hair carefully coiffed in a military ducktail, Private Fabian Lamanza glanced at the major, glanced up the road, glanced at the rifle in his hands, and decided that his uncle was gonna die.

It had been the old man's idea that Fabian join the army, learn something about life, learn a skill that had nothing to do with hubcaps, and return to Brooklyn a bona fide hero; it had been his idea that Fabian strengthen body and mind in order to stand up to the extortionist gangs that had just about taken over the neighborhood; it had been his effing brilliant idea not to join the navy because the navy always got itself into trouble someplace or another, and guys were always falling off ships and crashing into mountains and shit like that.

Fabian sneered and blew a smoke ring.

No question about it—as soon as he got outta this, he was taking the leave coming to him, and he was gonna skin the old man alive with a dull bayonet. Then he was gonna go AWOL, take over the Hot Devil Prongs, and rule Brooklyn for the rest of his natural life.

Screw it; this monster stuff was for the birds.

"Excuse me?"

"Yeah?"

"Are you a soldier?"

With a roll of his eyes, Fabian looked over his shoulder, a cutting remark at his lips.

It never came out.

He fell in love.

The cigarette fell in his lap.

"Yes, ma'am," he said, scrambling hastily to his feet and hoping the beautiful young woman smiling tenderly at him didn't mind that he had to make sure his balls weren't on fire.

She of the angelic countenance, swept-back black hair, and ass all jeans designers wept for at night, sighed. "Are we going to die?"

The major shouted.

"Not as long as I'm around," he boasted with a slap to the butt of his trusty, somewhat modified M-16.

Her smile became a mischievous grin. "Oh? And you think you can protect me, Private?"

"Fucking A," he said.

She giggled.

Fabian wished Ham were over here to see this.

"Well . . . hey, if you're going to make love to me, don't you think I should know your name?"

Shyly he told her, then stepped back a puzzled pace when he realized what she had said. Make love? He couldn't believe it. Nineteen years in Brooklyn and not a simple damn chick had ever propositioned him in such a classy way. Man, maybe his uncle had been right after all.

"Thank you," she said bashfully.

"Uh, I don't know yours," he said, hunting for his swagger.

"Kitty," she said. "Kitty O'Malley. My father's the editor of the newspaper."

Someone fired a rifle, Fabian leapt in front of Kitty and brought his rifle up, and Kitty whispered, "So when can I tell him we're going to be married?"

Reverend Phyllis Lager, clothing torn all to heck and face smeared with mud and dead leaves, stood in the backyard of her home and heaved a sigh at what was left of her house. It missed, but she didn't care. That grubby little corporal with the roving but not uninteresting hands had saved her life, and she had managed to make her way through the woods without once running into a ravenous bear.

She supposed she was lucky to be alive, even if the limousine was a total loss.

If only Phil, that reckless servant of the Lord, hadn't been so impulsive.

Slowly she made her way across the branch-and-blossom-strewn grass and around the house to the street, glanced once toward the center of town, and turned left, more limping than walking to a tall white steeple-shaped building on the corner. Thank the Lord, it was still in one piece. Of course, the neon cross no longer burned beaconlike above the roof, the neon face of Jesus no longer smiled benevolently down upon the neighborhood from above the simulated marble Ionic columns flanking the double simulated carved oak front doors, and the neon Crown of Eternal Thorns no longer glinted above the rose trestle arch at the foot of the walk that led to the front doors.

But that didn't matter either.

The roses were dead, but she was alive.

She was breathing.

She was able to sweat and pant and feel pain and sneeze and scratch at the gnat bites that covered her arms.

She was alive.

And she had seen the *Thing*!

If only Phil hadn't tried to convert it, had instead seen that the creature was not a creature of surpassing, indescribable Evil but a prophet sent to the Holy Spirit Today Tabernacle Society in order to ensure that it continue its good works and forecast the end of the world without being too specific about it . . . if only he had seen and known and felt all this, he wouldn't be dog meat right now.

And she wouldn't be alone.

All alone.

Staring at a distraught woman standing on the steps in torn jeans and wrinkled wimple.

"I have seen the Light!" the woman declared, her hands clasped to her bosom.

Phyllis stopped midway up the walk. "You've what?"

"I have seen the Rapture and the Light and the Power!"

Phyllis barely flinched when the roof of a house across the street suddenly bust into flame; she resisted turning her head when the cry of the Beast filled the fiery night; but she did take a step back when the woman ran down the steps toward her.

"Have you seen It?" the woman asked eagerly.

"Of course," Phyllis responded.

The woman spread her hands prayerfully. "It is a sign, don't you think? A revelation? An omen?"

Ever fearful of ecumenical sedition, Phyllis looked at her sideways. "You a Papist or something?"

The woman gave her a *what does it matter now?* look, and added, "It is the Dove in damned good disguise. It is the Message and the Messenger! It is . . . it *is*!"

Phyllis felt a tingling at the base of her spine. "You really think so?"

"I am Sister Lillian Vorth," the woman declared with humble pride. "I am never wrong about signs and other ecclesiastical manifestations of the Lord's work on this Earth of ours." She leaned forward. "I have seen Its work from afar." She lowered her voice. "In the space of one magnificent purple instant, Its power saved the soul of a woman of the night."

Phyllis blinked. "Are you sure?"

Sister Lillian nodded emphatically.

Then Phyllis, with insight so vivid she nearly lost her balance, recognized the nun, realized what a following the woman would generate with her piety and humble jeans, and grabbed her hands.

"They want to destroy It," she confided.

Sister Lillian gasped in horror.

"I was there. At the first battle. Hundreds of them. They tried to *kill* It!"

The nun hitched her jeans up, adjusted her wimple, and jutted her chin toward Main Street. "Then we must tell them before it's too late. We must show them that violence is not the answer. We must show them The Way!"

Relieved that she had found someone to take Phil's place so she wouldn't have to think so hard, Phyllis let the grateful tears flow, let the nun guide her back to the street. This, she knew, was her mission, her calling, the reason why Phil had been fried and the limo dented beyond repair; *this* was her life!

"Everything," said Sister Lillian as they rounded the corner at an evangelical trot.

"What?"

The nun smiled at her. "Everything. We must do everything in our power to be sure the heathens do not destroy our It."

And she didn't even blink when they heard the sudden gunfire.

"All right, that's better," the major said.

A crowd had gathered at her feet. The tired, the weary, the injured, the maimed, the bedraggled and the bedazzled, the bewildered and the bothered, were drawn to the tank and the vision of authority atop it. A few applauded. A few asked questions the major brushed away with a gesture. A woman with a broom suggested that this was hardly the time for speeches when, as rumor had it, there was a *Thing* from outer space on the outskirts of town.

The major glared her into silence.

"We have a situation here," she announced, in case there were a few who hadn't quite caught up with the rest of Gander Pond. "We have your basic alien creature invasion from Mars, which, if handled correctly, will be taken care of with acceptable losses and a promise of complete victory at the end."

A few in the back cheered.

"What we must do now is organize! Without organization, we are nothing, and we will be dead. Therefore, by the powers invested in me by the Uniform Code of Military Justice, the governor of this state, and the President of the United States, I am declaring martial law in Gander Pond!"

"You can't do that!" a pudgy man protested shrilly as he pushed his way through the stunned crowd. "I'm the mayor! You can't do that!"

The major looked down at him in more ways than one. "I see. And you are, I suppose, fully trained and equipped to take care of this situation?"

"I got a camera," he said, holding up an auto-focus, auto-flash, auto-wind, auto-zoom SLR. Another man slapped him on the back. "I got contacts with the networks. I got—"

"Private," the major said, "shoot him in the kneecaps."

Private Delphim lowered his rifle's aim.

Mayor Ellader backed away, but not before snapping a picture. "You haven't heard the end of this, Major!" he threatened. "I'll call my congressman."

The major addressed the crowd. "We must prepare a line of defense. We must arm all able-bodied citizens and place them on the rooftops, in the trees, in the doorways, in the streets." The crowd cheered. "We will devise a plan of hit-and-run, sniper attacks, and bold initiative. We must execute said plan to such a degree that that mother-hating *Thing* will wish it had never been born!" The crowd roared. "We will—"

"What about the tank?" a rumpled man with a piece of charcoal and a scrap of paper demanded.

The major glared at the editor who had screwed things up earlier. "What about it?"

"Was it used out there on Mountain Road?"

"Of course it was."

The editor licked the tip of the charcoal. "Did it stop the *Thing*?"

The crowd began to murmur.

"Private," the major said quietly.

Delphim aimed from the hip.

"Daddy, no!" a teenaged love interest screamed, and threw herself in front of her father and dared Delphim to shoot her first.

"Go ahead," the major said.

Delphim brought the rifle to his shoulder.

The crowd muttered.

An explosion more vicious than any other rocked the street, and someone screamed, "Oh, my *God*! It's got the Palace!"

It was then that the major realized she hadn't quite made her point.

"Reinforcements are coming!" she shouted over the hullabaloo. "Damnit, I've got reinforcements coming!"

"Who?" the emboldened mayor demanded caustically. "Him?"

He pointed.

The crowd looked.

The major turned and looked.

The soldiers stood in their places and looked.

Ham Delphim peered around the tank and looked.

And there, streaking down the road, was a neon-red car with a man on the roof, holding on to a rack of antlers and waving a rifle as if his life, and that of the entire planet, depended on it.

"Private," the major said, "shoot that sonofabitch."

· 2 ·

When Chita screamed for the eighth time since leaving the
parking lot—something about turning on the headlights, you
idiot, don't you know it's dark out—Kent decided he had had
quite enough of her whining. After all, potential world destruction or no potential world destruction, it was his bloody
car and his bloody driving skills, and if she didn't like either
she could get the hell out and wait for Hooker and the hooker.
It was, in fact, on the tip of his tongue to say several scathing
words to that effect when, in an apparent fit of front-seat
driving, she seized his right arm.

"Hey!" he shouted.

"Hey yourself!" she shouted back, and pointed at the large
ragged crater that had appeared somewhat abruptly in the
middle of the road some fifty yards down the way. It smoked.
It burned. It cast clumps and gobs of black stuff and stones
into the air. And Kent swerved sharply to the right to avoid
plunging into its depths.

"Damnit, woman, if you hadn't—"

Chita screamed again.

This time, he had no time for chastisement. He was far too
busy avoiding the much too solid-looking trees that lined the
verge onto whose graveled surface he had been forced in order not to crash into the hole. Brake and steer, brake and
steer, and it was all so confusing that he steered and braked
before he realized what he was doing and immediately found
himself stalled in a shallow ditch directly parallel to the hole.

118

For a long moment there was silence.

Then Chita said, "Are you all right?"

Shakily he nodded.

She hit him.

As best he could within the confines of the steering wheel, he twisted about with fierce determination and swore in ancient Gaelic when she scrambled out of the Dilemma, trailing ammo belts and a machine gun and a few words of Spanish origin which, while not easily translatable, left no doubt about where he sat in her scheme of things. He glared. He grabbed his rifle. He lunged out of the car just as a searing red beam smokily trimmed the edges of the hole, the aftermath of which was a subsonic boom that knocked him on his ass.

"You all right?" she asked, crouched by the rear fender.

"Don't hit," he warned.

She laughed. "Why should I, when that thing is going to fry your royal *cajones*?"

A swift examination of the automobile proved that it was in decent working order, neither disastrously mired nor immobile, just stalled; a quicker examination of the highway they'd just left proved that the *Thing* which had been stalking them had inexplicably halted its relentless progress toward Gander Pond. Swathed in billows of steam and smoke, trees aflame on either side, it seemed to be fascinated by the Gander Palace. One might even imagine it to be anthropomorphically bemused by the unusual structure.

"Chita," he whispered, "we can't stay here." Cautiously, so as not to draw the creature's attention to them, he opened the passenger door and pointed. "Get in. Start the engine. I'll push until you're free."

"No fighting?" she said.

A careless red beam cut a perfect Z into the parking lot.

"Lords are pretty smart," she allowed.

"Baron," he corrected wearily, then grabbed her arm just as she prepared to make her leap into the car.

"What? What?" she demanded.

He pointed up the road.

There, emerging from the smoke, were Casopia and Nick. On foot. Clothing in tatters. Choking. Coughing. So badly ragged that Hooker's sleeves had somehow been obscenely rolled down to his wrists. In addition, the scientist limped badly and leaned heavily on the woman.

"Oh boy," Chita observed prophetically.

At the same time, the visually but not totally obscured *Thing* noticed the Palace refugees.

A low rumble rolled ominously across the valley.

"We have to do something," Kent said. "My Lord, we must do something!"

Casopia noticed the beast's notice and tried to run, but Hooker's weight and injurious condition prevented everything but a lame trot.

"Run!" Chita screamed.

"Not exactly what I had in mind," Kent muttered, and began a semi-crouched sprint along the rocky bottom of the ditch. He hoped the creature would be so enthralled by the helplessness of his latest victims that it would not see him until it was too late.

Too late for what? he asked himself.

He was answered by an unsettling silence.

When next he looked, Casopia was less than five yards from the ditch and the dubious safety of the forest beyond.

"Gogogogogogo!" Chita bellowed.

Kent's finger twitched on the trigger.

Three yards.

Two yards.

And a scarlet heat ray sliced through the smoke, shimmering to dust a stately evergreen, splintering an oak, and gouging a rut not ten feet from the fleeing pair.

Casopia did not waver, though it seemed to Kent that Hooker had changed his mind and was trying to put on the brakes.

Then he heard shouting and chanced a look over his shoulder.

And gasped.

Chita had taken a defiant stance in the center of the road, machine gun at her practiced hip, ammunition belt slung over her right shoulder. She shouted again, attempting to draw the monster's attention. When that failed, and Kent tripped over a fallen branch, she fired.

The volley was deafening.

Her aim, judging by the red tracers interspaced with the bullets, was true.

But the *Thing* merely burped a moderate burst of return ray fire in her direction, spraying her with molten stone and revitalized tar, which sent her, in turn, shrieking invectively back into the ditch.

Kent ran on.

Casopia stumbled, fell, and Hooker rolled onto his back.

From the smoke, from the fury, from the soiled and tainted air, came a triumphant bellow . . . and what most certainly had to be a huge feathered foot, unless the feathers were actually long strands of lavender and lilac fur stiffened by the blood of many innocent soldiers.

Kent rose.

Casopia pulled desperately at Hooker's shoulders.

Chita threw a rock.

Kent set the rifle to his shoulder, prayed that the trigger worked, and squeezed it.

Then the foot, or the paw, wavered perceptibly before slamming onto the ground. But that slim hesitation was sufficient for Casopia to yank her man clear, haul him to her shoulders in a fireman's carry, and lumber off into the trees. Just before she disappeared, she glanced back.

Kent lowered his rifle and gave her a jaunty salute.

With an amused tilt of her head, she waved, picked up Hooker again, and vanished into the dark.

The *Thing* shot a broad-based vermilion heat ray after her, but it was too late, especially for the white birch saplings which had hitherto huddled behind the stately evergreen.

It grumbled.

And Kent dropped to the ground as its head swiveled ominously toward him.

Artie Chong, convinced that he would never wok again, nearly fell out of his saddle when he heard a monstrous explosion off to the south. Yet he dared not look over his shoulder. This horse, this beast, this indefatigable and thoroughly amazing animal, demanded all his attention.

It leapt over obstacles with effortless ease.

It flew around those it could not leap with a grace that brought a catch to his throat.

And it paid absolutely no attention to the commands he sent it by either rein, knee, toe, or fist.

It was, he thought with a shudder of superstition, almost as if it knew exactly where to go.

Which was at least a good mile and a half ahead of his own knowledge of the terrain. In fact, the major with the soft lips and hot breath hadn't given him precise instructions at all. She had only told him that he would know it when he found it, and since she had spent more time with the palomino than with him, he could only assume that she had somehow psychically communicated directions to it.

He had to assume so.

It was Gander Pond's only hope.

Thus did he ride onward into the ever darkening night, hearing the sound effects of battle grow faint in his wake, seeing only the stars and the weekend traffic grow more vivid straight ahead.

And just when he had closed his eyes in anticipation of a prodigious vault of a stalled eighteen-wheeler, the palomino swerved off the highway onto a narrow dirt road.

Branches whipped overhead; shadows paced him; through gaps in the blurred trunks on his right he could see a meadow's expanse, and on his left, the moonlit glitter of a small lake.

Sophia, he thought; oh, Sophia, I'm lost.

The horse whickered and shook its head.

Artie swept tangles of mane from his eyes and realized that the animal had slowed to an anxious canter.

"We here?" he asked of the darkness around him.

The palomino snorted.

Artie blinked.

The road darted unexpectedly to the left, ending just as unexpectedly at a tall wooden gate wrapped in barbed wire.

"Oh, don't," he pleaded as his mount picked up speed. "Oh, don't, please don't do—"

The palomino leapt.

And Artie Chong lost his grip.

Bleeding, bruised, and battered beyond anything she had ever experienced, including the one-eyed sailor from Bayonne, Casopia lowered herself wearily to the ground behind a sheltering boulder and carefully lay Hooker's head in her lap.

She leaned back and closed her eyes.

Sleep was all she wanted now. Sleep, and a hand-held nuclear bomb.

Hooker coughed.

She tried to wipe the dirt and blood from his brow, but succeeded only in smearing it into a perversion of mud.

"Casopia?" he whispered.

"Right here," she assured him.

"I have something to tell you."

Funny, she thought, how things work out. A guy braves the most disgusting threat to the world since spangled tights, dares to confront his dream face to whatever, and ends up with a stubbed toe that puts him flat on his back. She supposed it was better than a bullet in the head, but somehow the romance had leaked out of this adventure.

"Can you hear me?" he gasped.

She nodded when he opened his pleading eyes.

There they were, right behind that stupid red car with the horns on top, and Nick suddenly turns right instead of left, shouting above the noise of the wind that he had a theory he simply had to test or he wouldn't be able to live with himself in the morning. When, clinging to the back of her seat and watching Kent and the Latin tramp speed off toward safety, she reminded him that it was, in the first place, already morning, and in the second place, he wasn't in his laboratory, he had only patted her knee and aimed straight for the *Thing* she could sort of see in the midst of all that smoke.

She had weakened, and screamed.

He had obviously misunderstood and patted her knee again.

This time she made sure he knew what she was screaming about, but by then it was too late.

"I know," Hooker said from her lap. "You must listen to me, my darling. I know."

"Know what?" she asked. "What do you know?"

Something she had asked herself not thirty minutes before, when he laughed at her fears, laughed at the smoke that had enveloped the little sports car, and laughed when someone damned large and furry sideswiped the passenger side and sent them into a spin that landed them in a ditch.

Miraculously they had escaped unscathed.

Until something else awfully huge and probably hairy swung at them from the mist, and in turning to run, Hooker kicked a rock. Fell into a ditch. And had to lean on her in order to walk.

"Casopia, are you listening to me?"

She smiled vacantly.

Mindful of his injured toe, he sat up, combed his hair with his fingers, rolled his sleeves back up, and dusted his white shoes with one elbow. "You haven't heard a single word I've said," he complained.

"You haven't said much," she told him.

His tanned and dirty forehead wrinkled in a frown. "You mean, in my delirium I didn't explain?"

"Explain what?"

"Why, how to kill the monster, that's what."

Milos Athnos staggered purposefully down the white line of the highway. In one hand he held two grenades, in the other two rifles, and in his teeth a bayonet.

The tracks of the *Thing* were easy to follow.

But even if they hadn't been, he would have found it. Somehow. Some way.

Nobody killed his best friend and got away with it; nobody offed Master Sergeant Wagoneer without dealing with the Greek fury of the avenging corporal.

He licked his lips in anticipation, paying no heed to the blood that ran from the sudden wound in his tongue. It was nothing compared to what he was going to do when he met up with his destiny.

He hoped no one else would be around.

It was going to be ugly.

Little Janis Ellader, not wanting to help her mommy chase after Uncle Bill after the mortuary flooded, sat on the front porch of her father's mayoral home and petted the head of her cute little puppy, Sparky, a wire-haired terrier that had a craving for socks and dachshunds.

At each distant explosion, at each trembling of the ground, Sparky trembled and whined.

"It's all right, Sparky," Janis told him, hugging him tightly. "Don't be afraid."

Sparky wagged its stubby little tail.

A flare hovered over the town.

"Pretty," Janis said.

Sparky barked in agreement.

"Hey, Sparky," she said when another explosion slid her down a couple of steps, "I have a neat idea!"

The dog bounded to the lawn and barked.

"That's right! Let's go see that bad old monster. Maybe we can help Mommy and Daddy get rid of it."

The dog growled.

"Or maybe," the little girl added, "maybe we can make it a friend and they won't have to do bad things to it like they did to our ant farm."

Sparky yipped in agreement.

Janis stood, red hair and freckles just too adorable for words in the flickering nightmarish light, and, with a solemn nod to her loyal pet, started down the street.

Directly toward the edge of town.

Kent, puffing and wishing that invasions weren't quite so enervating, once again assumed a minimum target stance and rushed to the spot where Chita had thrown herself wantonly into the ditch. When he arrived in a slide that took him to her side, she threw her arms around him and held on, trembling, murmuring, finally lifting her head and saying, "That was a pretty brave thing you done back there, Baron."

"It didn't feel brave," he admitted. "It felt rather stupid, if you must know."

She grinned, and kissed him quickly. "Y'know, you ain't too bad for a guy that ain't in my class."

He considered several appropriately gallant replies, but none of them exposed themselves because they were both abruptly thrown onto their backs as a result of a blast that took them by surprise.

"God *damn!*" Chita said, quickly sitting up and brushing debris from her hair and chest.

"Perhaps," Kent answered, and painfully swiveled around to see that the visitor from beyond the ionosphere had evidently decided to take out the loss of two more victims on the Palace.

On his home.

"Aw shit," he said.

From the depths of the yellow and orange smoke, from the Hell that spun in whorls and nebulae around it, the *Thing* used all the powers at its command to take apart the luxury pyramid building brick by stone, window by joist.

A ray sizzled along the foundation, melting everything in its path; a beam punched at the remaining panes, sending glass spiraling and screaming into the air like downed jet fighters; a knife blade of heat slammed into the third story and produced a gap large enough to cause the floor above to begin a slow, inexorable collapse; a serrated or possibly saw-toothed horn or tooth tore off ironwork railings as if they were paper; a paw or a foot or some part of a prehensile tail cleaned out the lobby in a single, damnably effective swing.

Sparks danced and soared.

Fires ignited and puffed as all combustible material within the battered walls were touched by the rays and the beams and the visible strokes of heat.

A man ran around the corner of the dying building and was turned to ash before he could leap to safety over the back fence; a woman and her corgi became fiery reminders of the creature's hatred of all mankind; an automobile shuddered and blew up, thus blowing up at least a dozen others in its row; a fleeing parrot became a Brazilian flare.

And then, just as Kent wondered what was holding the building together, the *Thing* lanced its devilish weapon at the top floor.

"Jesus!" he yelled, and threw himself over Chita.

"You baron guys really got lousy timing, you know?" she said before her eyes widened in terror, her mouth opened in fear, and he could feel the scream coming. In a desperate effort to prevent the creature from learning of their location, Kent planted his lips solidly upon hers. He knew what was about to happen; he could think of worse ways to die. Not many. But a few.

Casopia's armory blew up.

No national celebration could hold a candle to it.

No natural destructive force had ever displayed such power.

Every rocket was launched, every bullet fired, every arrow and sword and knife blasted into the sky, every mine exploded, every bomb detonated. A streaking, multicolored, expanding pillar of pure fire and smoke mushroomed toward the stars, flaming bits and pieces showering everywhere, turning trees to torches and grass to hot plates.

The noise concussed.

The light blinded.

The air filled with the shrapnel of a hundred lost lives and condominia.

Time froze.

The *Thing* stomped its appendages in glee.

And Kent pulled back when the initial effects had settled into a steady roar, took a deep breath, and looked at what was left of his mortgage.

There was nothing but flame and soot.

Even the *Thing* seemed stunned by the consequence of its assault.

At last, Kent said, ''C'mon,'' and yanked Chita to her feet.

Puzzled at his tone, she looked at him, looked at the results of the monster's fury, and a curious expression of disappointment flickered over her face before, snapping herself out of it, she nodded.

''Hey,'' he said as she scrambled inside, retrailing her ammo belts and machine gun, ''you know how to drive?''

A glare of disgust was her answer. But this wasn't just any car in any mildly dangerous situation he was entrusting to her; this was the only thing he had left in the world aside from the clothes on his back. He wasn't about to let her—

The *Thing* laughed and spat flame over its shoulder.

Kent instantly tossed his rifle into the car, nodded when she seated herself behind the wheel, and closed the door softly.

The *Thing* began to work on what remained in the parking lot.

Fire lit the post-midnight sky. Shadows climbed the Palace's walls.

As Kent positioned himself for a manly push, Chita started the engine and drove out of the ditch.

The *Thing* swung its ponderous upper portions around and blindly blasted the ditch.

Kent, too astonished to move, felt the intraspacial heat
beam whiz past his ear and torch the nearest conifer. When
the next one opened a crater less than six inches from where
he stood, he leapt onto the blacktop and began running,
screaming at Chita to slow the hell down.

She did, but only long enough for him to fling himself onto
the car trunk and cling spread-eagled to it. Then she was off
again, gears grinding, engine whining, veering expertly side
to side to avoid the deadly red beam popping chuckholes in
their wake.

Kent closed his eyes and inched his way forward until he
could precariously fingertip-grip the pitted frame of the rear
window and look through to the front. Chita waggled her
fingers at him in the rearview mirror and veered again. His
legs swung across the trunk. A ray singed off his antlers.
Chita zigged and zagged, and Kent, as he rolled from one
fender to the other, zagged sharply, and knew with Celtic
certainty that he would never make it to Gander Pond alive.
If the woman he had impulsively proposed to didn't kill him
with her evasive tactics, the *Thing* being evaded would probably boil his blue blood.

Another explosion some forty yards ahead.

Without hesitation, Chita drove straight through the acrid
green smoke and used a propitious upcropping of blacktop to
launch the car into the air and over the new hole.

Kent sobbed when he felt the ground suddenly drop away;
he moaned when the ground returned with a crash that rattled
his stomach; and swore mightily, if ineffectively, when his
grip began to slip.

The situation was intolerable. But as he discovered, again,
that he didn't want to die, there was nothing for it but a
reckless, onetime move that would alone decide his fate.

He took a deep breath.

He gathered the remnants of his strength and used them to
pummel his fear into submission.

Then, before he could think about what he was doing and
what would happen if he didn't do it right, he lunged forward,
shoes scraping neon paint, fingers scrabbling, mouth open in
a soundless bellow of self-support, until, the wind punishing
his hair, he grabbed the rearmost antlers with one clawing
hand and prayed they were sturdy enough to hold him.

For several death-tempting seconds he clung there, body whipped back and forth, mind seeking blessed oblivion.

For several more seconds he felt his grip begin to lose its tenacity.

No, he thought; not this far and no farther; gimme a break.

He hauled, he kicked, he scraped, he grabbed, and despite all the odds and Chita's increasingly erratic driving, he found himself sprawled on the roof, propped on the antlers as the car hurtled toward the growing lights of Gander Pond.

It wasn't pretty, but it definitely beat the alternative.

He rapped the windshield to signal her he was all right.

Chita honked the horn in celebration.

And with unerring accuracy, the *Thing* snickered a laser-thin ray that blew out the left rear tire.

The car lurched, but Chita masterfully maintained control, rounding a bend that opened the road up into a straightway that led directly into Main Street.

Eyes tearing from the wind, Kent saw dark houses flash past, saw that many of the streetlamps had been turned back on, and saw a barricade of five Jeeps and a tank dead ahead.

He pulled himself up and waved his rifle in glee.

Chita honked the horn and flashed the lights.

And a short guy stepped around one of the vehicles and raised a rifle to his shoulder.

Holy cow, Kent thought in disbelief, that little prick is going to kill me!

· 3 ·

In fear for their lives, Casopia and Nicodemus huddled cheek-to-cheek against the boulder that had been their refuge when the *Thing*, as far as they could tell, began tearing apart the universe. Chips of stone, splinters of wood, and bits of soft pinkish things showered around them, while sparks touched off tiny fires on the ground and in the foliage. To protect them, however feebly, Hooker shrugged out of his lavender jacket and draped it tentlike over their heads, enfolded her once more in his arms, and patted and rubbed her back until she felt as if she ought to either burp or throw up.

The ensuing bedlam caused by the assault prevented their speaking.

She didn't mind.

Her ears hurt anyway, and it gave her a chance to mull over his last words.

Kill that critter? Could he really do it? Had his intuitive, scientifically bent mind actually seen through the monster's invincible facade, or was it just the agony of his afflicted foot?

She burped.

And halfway through a mental thank-you note to the butler for saving their lives, an earth-shattering explosion split their boulder down the middle and showered them with rock dust. Instantly they were on their feet and racing deeper into the woods, a distance of approximately ten feet before the concussion knocked them to the ground.

Nuts, she thought as she spotted a rocket's red glare burst in the heavens; there goes the good stuff.

The quiet that followed was eerie, almost preternatural. For several minutes, all they could hear was the rainlike patter of debris falling through the trees, their own ragged breathing, and the muffled snorting of the *Thing*, as if it were both stunned and confused by what it had done.

"Are you all right?" Hooker asked, turning his head toward her without getting up.

A quick check of all limbs and increasingly exposed flesh, and she decided that she was, under the circumstances, more alive than dead.

"Wonderful." Hooker sat up gingerly. "I think now would be the best time to see if my theory is correct."

Personally she didn't think so. Not only had they lost their weapons, they had also lost their transportation, their possibility of salvation, and very likely his mind.

Oblivious to her doubts, Hooker nodded thoughtfully. "Yes." He cupped one ear to better listen to the beast's curious breathing. "Yes, I do think this is definitely the only chance we're going to get."

He stood and faced the highway.

Casopia sat up. "Nick, what the hell are you talking about?"

"The killing method," he said somberly. "I believe I have devised the only weapon we on Earth have to defeat this thing."

"I thought you wanted to talk about it."

"It wrecked my car." He looked down at her sadly. "You wouldn't understand, my dear, but my life has been really rotten from childhood until now, and all I ever wanted since I was a lad, aside from the pursuit of my lifelong dream, was that little red two-seater sports car." His blue eyes narrowed dangerously. "When your dreams come in conflict with your reality, Casopia, sometimes the dream loses."

She nodded, reached out, and waited for him to help her to her feet.

He pointed toward the highway. "My dream out there has just totaled my other dream. The bastard."

She shook her arm.

"I may be a civilized man, Casopia, but I do have my limits."

She cleared her throat.

He brushed a dead leaf from his wrinkled, pale yellow shirt, and absently dusted his grass-and-gravel-stained white trousers. "I shall teach him how man deals with those who tamper with the only things we hold more sacred than our mothers—our dreams."

Abandoning hope of chivalry, she sprang effortlessly to her feet and held his arm in sympathy. "Nick, that's no dream out there, that's a nightmare."

"So it is," he agreed, with the air of a man who has just opened the shades in the morning and discovered that his garbage can was the only one left that hadn't been emptied. Again. "So it is."

With another adjustment to his hair, he began a swift march toward the road. Casopia, torn between her infatuation with this strange but lovable person, and her deep and abiding worship of life as she knew it, vacillated only a few seconds before hurrying after him.

"How are you going to do it?" she asked when she had caught up.

He smiled at her. "At the last, it was elementary."

She grinned. "You're going to deduce him to death?"

His laugh was quick and sweet, and she felt a sudden tug at her heart, the most dangerous position a woman like her could find herself in, next to being blindfolded on a greased trapeze held by an amorous Shriner.

"By any chance," he said, wiping his eyes free of mirth, "did you hear what the *Thing* said just before we escaped into these woods?"

"Said?" She stared in astonishment. "Said?"

"Yes. Said."

She was about to remind him that terrifically pissed-off monsters from beyond the moon did not say anything; they just tromped around as if they owned the place. But the words were never formed, because, suddenly and with a gasp of recognition, she did remember something.

At the time, she had thought it was her natural hysteria and concern and terror which distorted the sounds the beast was making. Surely they couldn't have been words. English words.

That was clearly impossible, and so her mind had blamed it on the heat of the moment.

"Ah," said the scientist, "I see that you first believed you were hearing things."

"Well, I was," she said, stepping around what she thought might be one of her pillows, "but not words."

"Ah, but they were."

She almost laughed.

He was absolutely serious.

"Nick, are you sure?"

"Tell me what you thought you heard," he encouraged as he kicked aside a charred fragment of young King Tut's left iris.

"I can't," she demurred. "I feel silly."

"Oh, go ahead," he urged.

"Well . . ." She giggled. She chuckled. She cleared her throat, deepened her voice, cupped her hands around her mouth, and said, "I'm coming, Beany, I'm coming!" Then she laughed so hard she nearly tripped over a rock that turned out to be either someone's overdone head, or a rock. She sobered instantly and stared at Hooker. "But . . . but . . ."

"No buts about it," he assured her.

And she listened with blossoming astonishment and awe as he explained how, in the past of not too long ago, a great many reputable scientists had pooh-poohed the outmoded notion that a nation's broadcasts, whether they be television or radio signals, not only reached the devices for which they had been originally intended but also escaped the Earth's atmosphere and were, even now, forever traveling through the dark reaches of space. He was not a pooh-pooher. He was a proponent of precisely that which had so long been pooh-poohed. It is therefore, he continued, more than conceivable that an advanced race on an advanced planet just might intercept these broadcasts and, after many decades of careful and intense study, deduce that the signals were, indeed, clear manifestations of speech patterns. From this they just might extrapolate the existence of another civilization living elsewhere in the galaxy. And from that, they might, were they imaginative enough, use those selfsame broadcasts to learn the language and thus speculate on the lives and loves of a perhaps unreachable people.

"In a way," he concluded as they approached the edge of the forest, "it's rather sad."

The skunklike aroma of recent battle soured Casopia's reaction to his Romanticism; nevertheless, she found the entire hypothesis difficult to swallow.

"You mean that son of a bitch learned English from television shows?"

"Only the audio, my dear. Anything else would be silly."

He dropped to his hands and knees then, and indicated that she should follow suit. When she had, he crawled her silently to a smoldering bush at the edge of the roadside ditch. Then he peered around the smoky branches and nodded, took a pen from his shirt pocket, and began doodling on the warm, scorched earth as he muttered to himself.

Casopia looked around her side of their cover and clamped a hand over her mouth in order to stifle a cry of dismay.

The Gander Palace was gone.

The parking lot was gone.

Everything was gone except the *Thing*, which stood in a thinning cloud of smoke in the middle of the road, slapping itself roughly.

Hooker looked up absently when she tapped his shoulder. "Simply an interstellar method of ridding the cobwebs," he explained, and returned to his doodling. "Nothing to worry about."

Incredible, she thought.

"So what are you going to do?" she whispered. "Commercial it to death?"

He rocked back on his heels and stabbed the pen at the equations he had created, lips pursed solemnly. "I don't think so. I rather suspect commercials would only either put him to sleep temporarily or bore him silly enough to make him lose his temper and start smashing things again. No. Something a bit more daring is required. You see, I believe that he, or she, has been subliminally conditioned by exposure to those sound waves, and thus rendered violent, thus murderous, thus an efficient and remorseless killing machine." He shook his head in admiration. "Incredible."

"A killer?" she said. "That giant toad was made a killer by *Beany and Cecil*?"

Hooker closed one eye and regarded their adversary. "Well,

in the first place, I hardly think toad describes that creature. There are too many—''

With a strangled cry of exasperation, she grabbed his shoulders and shook him. ''Who gives a shit, you pea-brained hunk? Are you going to kill it or what? Good Lord, as soon as that slime bucket recovers, it's going to squash Gander Pond and everyone in it.''

His mouth opened, closed, opened again. ''You're right. This is no time for petty disagreements.'' He rose and adjusted his lapels. ''Wish me luck.''

''What?'' In panic and disbelief, she scrambled to her feet and threw her arms around his waist. ''Nick, what the hell do you think you're doing?''

''Why, I'm going out there to kill it.''

''How?''

He whistled a tune that made her frown in its familiarity, then kissed her passionately before moving her aside and scrambling down into the shallow ditch and up the other side before she could recover.

''Nick!'' she called, no longer caring if the *Thing* could hear her.

He waved without looking.

The *Thing* heard her and began to turn.

But Nicodemus Hooker faced his dream and whistled on.

Benny Hart vowed on the liberation army Code of Conduct for General Gain that the next time he had the chance to become involved with a mountain woman, he wasn't going to. At least not this one. MaryLou Krutch was too headstrong, too much her own boss, and even though she had trusted him to bring up the rear, he knew that her night-trained eyes were keeping careful track of him.

As if she thought he might turn tail and run.

He sneered in her general direction, slapped aside a branch that wanted to give him a new eye, and trudged up the slope. He carried a flashlight larger than his forearm, and two shovels and a pick were strapped across his back. Smith, in the middle, carried a canvas sack filled with food. MaryLou, now rounding a cage of birch, carried a rifle, a handgun, a flashlight, and four empty bags for, she said, the booty.

The purple glow faded.

Gander Mountain grew darker.

To make sure the alien wasn't following them, Benny whirled about every few yards and stabbed his light at the trail below. So far, he considered himself lucky—all he'd surprised were two dead possums, a raccoon, and something that might have been an owl with a rat in its beak. He didn't like owls; their heads turned funny. He didn't like rats either, so he guessed he came out ahead of something or other, though he wasn't sure he was thinking very straight at the moment.

It was the smell wafting from the summit that confused him.

A curious smell, much like a cauldron of boiling honey that had been laced with caramel and raspberry jam. It was so overpowering, it turned his stomach and made his teeth ache, but he would be damned if he was going to show weakness now. They had come too far, and risked too much, for him to prove the weak link in the expedition's chain.

"How much farther?" Smith gasped.

Benny didn't hear MaryLou's answer, but the way the strange man suddenly picked up the pace, he didn't think they would be much longer.

He certainly hoped not.

One of those dead possums had tried to bite off his ankle.

The purple glow faded.

The flashlights jabbed the dark away.

MaryLou chopped aside a pine branch, laced into a thicket of stubborn ferns, and called back, "You'd better move it, boys, because you ain't gonna believe this."

Benny hurried up to the ridge she had topped, and lost his breath, as if someone had punched him.

"Damn," he said.

"Damn," Smith echoed.

"Army," said MaryLou, "I think we just found our retirement fund."

When the palomino landed cleanly on the other side of the wooden gate, Artie slid off its back and tumbled into a hummock, came up against a bone-hard tree trunk, and lay there, staring at the sky and hoping that the damned horse would break a leg, maybe even its neck. Mission of mercy or not, he was beginning to feel a little bit used.

The horse trotted back and whickered at him.

The tree trunk moved.

Artie shifted his gaze upward.

"Well," he said after a full minute of concentration.

"You alive?" the tree asked.

Artie smiled wanly and rolled into a kneeling position. He rubbed at several bodily locations bruised in the fall while muttering a complicated recipe for Zen fried chicken in order to maintain his inner equilibrium.

"If you're alive," the tree informed him, "then I am under orders to shoot you for trespassing on secret government property."

Inhaling sharply, Artie rocked unsteadily to his feet and held out his hands in supplication. "Please," he pleaded, "do not shoot. I came . . . I have . . . There is . . . a message for your . . . commanding officer."

"Oh, really?" the tree said skeptically.

"Yes. And I am supposed to give the code of the day to the guard on duty." He squinted. "Are you the guard on duty?"

The tree grunted assent. "But make it quick, shortie. I still gotta shoot you."

Praying swiftly to his beloved Sophia for the strength to be brazen without being offensive, Artie lifted his chin bravely and said, "Sea gull."

The tree rustled in astonishment. "Say . . . what?"

"No," said Artie impatiently. "Sea gull."

The tree shivered. "Son of a bitch."

Artie tapped his foot, snapped his fingers, listened as a crank turned, a buzzer buzzed, and the tree mumbled something into a knothole. Come on, he thought; come on, white boy, move your khaki ass.

Then the tree stepped out of the dark and ordered Artie to follow him. And as they hurried down a narrow, rutted path, the tree said, "So hey, we really being attacked by an invader from Mars?"

With righteous murder in his heart, Milos rounded the bend in the highway and stopped with a sharp inhalation.

Directly ahead was the *Thing* he had been stalking.

He snarled.

He prepared a swift strategy of charge and destruction, and
was about to shift himself into automatic so he wouldn't have
to think about his possible demise when, suddenly, he put
everything on hold.

There was a man down there.

A goddamned man dressed like a Florida real estate agent,
standing bold as brass in front of the *Thing*, which was looking down at him with no less than an alien expression of both
amusement and puzzlement.

Shit, Milos thought.

And the stranger, incredibly, put his hands on his hips.

Benny scrambled down into the crater caused by the spacecraft's crash landing. The others followed, deferring to him,
since it was his idea in the first place. He suspected they were
also wary of booby traps, other aliens, and such, but his
expert liberation gaze told him in a fraction of a second that
whatever had flown to Earth in this thing had had no time to
worry about securing its perimeter.

Either that, or it plain didn't care.

"My, my," he said.

The sides of the upthrust excavation were not all that steep,
but they were pocked with steaming holes and strewn with
unearthed rocks, hunks of molten earth, debarked boles, a
tail or two, and gnarled branches sucked off their trees by the
vortex of the passing crash.

It was a vision of Hell, with lots of smoke and stuff.

Benny gazed at the wreck with both dread and grudging
respect.

If the craft had indeed used a saucer configuration, or even
a small teakettle, there was no sign of it now. From what he
could see, most of it had been buried by the force of its
landing; what remained aboveground in the mist and the dark
were great curves and arcs and arches and sweeps and planes
and spirals of a metal such as he had never seen before in his
life. It glowed. It pulsed. It emitted a curious humming sound.
Here and there spouted tongues of steam. Over there was a
lick of fire. Nearer to his feet, along the sleek and pitted side
of the spacecraft, a confusing hieroglyphic sequence which
may or may not have been the spaceship's name or identifi-
cation number.

"You think we can get inside, army?" MaryLou asked, her voice hushed.

He shrugged. "Don't see a hatch."

"Then how did the thing get out?"

"Here," Smith answered. He stood by a jutting fin cracked raggedly in half. "Looks like . . . here."

Benny made his way over, taking care not to slip on the slope and slide into the side. He had no idea how hot the metal was, and he did not, now or ever, want to find out.

Smith leaned forward, squinted, and pointed. "I can see pipes and wires and things. It must have gotten out here right after it crashed." He straightened and shook his head in astonishment. "My lord, it's a wonder it wasn't killed."

"You know something?" MaryLou said as Benny approached the breach cautiously. "The ass end of this thing looks like the '59 Caddy convertible my uncle once had. It wasn't purple, though, it was pink." She blew out a breath. "Ugliest damned thing you ever saw in your life."

A cloud of steam abruptly escaped from the rent, and the two men fell onto their backs in fear and surprise.

"Maybe it's going to blow up," Smith said.

"Don't think so," Benny told him.

"You think we can—"

Suddenly MaryLou cried out in pain, and Benny whirled just in time to see her flail her arms and fall heavily to the ground. He jumped and pushed and fought to her side, helped her to sit up, and was about to ask her what had happened when he spotted something lying on the ground.

"Wow," he said, kneeling over it and poking at it with a stick. "Wow."

"Don't touch it," she warned nervously. "Damn thing knocked me over."

He smiled an *of course it did* and aimed his flashlight at it.

Smith joined them. "What's that, a gun?"

Working with an archaeologist's care, Benny brushed away the dirt that clung to the artifact's sides, used MaryLou's Bowie knife to dig a trench around it, then sat back and said, "Yeah, I think you're right."

"Man," said MaryLou.

Smith just watched.

A moment later, the mountain was rocked by an immense explosion that lit up the sky, flared off the spaceship's side and fins and arcs and arches, and set the steam vents around the craft to working full-time.

The three looked westward.

"Sounds like heap big trouble," MaryLou guessed soberly.

"I don't think they can beat it," Benny agreed.

They exchanged a glance, stared at the weapon, and nodded to each other.

But Smith was too fast. He darted between them, snatched up the weapon, and pointed it at their chests when they made a move to seize him.

"Don't make me do it," he warned.

"Do what?" Benny asked.

"Kill you."

"What the hell would you do that for?"

Smith grinned maniacally. "This," he said, "is going to make me rich again."

"Fiddle," said MaryLou. "He don't know how to use it, army. No sweat."

Benny agreed and reached out for it.

Smith slapped a button, yanked a lever, and a thin blue beam hummed out of some part of what he held, striking Benny's left leg.

Benny yelled and fell to his knees, yelled and fell onto his back, sat up and looked down at his leg. There was a hole in his pants. There was a hole in his leg.

MaryLou leaned over to examine it. "Man, you can see right through that sucker, army. Cauterized it and everything. It hurt?"

"I don't know," he said. "Sort of. A little."

"Get up!" Smith ordered. "You're not dead."

"Shut up!" MaryLou retorted.

But Benny had spotted the madness in the man's bleary eyes and knew it would do no good to attempt reason with him, whether he understood the weapon's articulation or not. Stiffly, and with MaryLou's help, he made it back to his feet.

Smith chuckled. "Rich. Rich." He shook a filthy fist at the sky. "Damn you, Samantha and Georgette, you're going to pay for it now!" He laughed; he cried; he laughed again and burned a hole in MaryLou's pheasant feather when she tried to sneak up and disarm him.

"Rich," Benny said. "Rich? What are you talking about, man? We got to bring that thing down to the army. We'll all die otherwise."

"Army's right," MaryLou agreed. "Can't sell none of this good stuff to no tourists if there ain't anyone around to be a tourist."

"I don't care!" Smith snarled. He began to drool a little from one corner of his trembling lips. "You have no idea what it's like to be treated like a bum. You have no idea what it's like to have your own father and mother disown you and your sisters call you nasty names!" He laughed. "You don't know! You can't know!" He laughed again. "But now . . . now I'm going to get even."

"How?" Benny asked, morbidly fascinated by this man's swift descent into insanity.

"I'm going to Long Island, that's how!" Smith declared with an evil cackle. "I'm going to blow that sonofabitch mansion all the goddamn way to New Haven, and then let's see who the black sheep in the family is, eh? Let's see who's sorry now, right? Let's see who has the last—"

He grunted.

His eyes popped.

His lips stopped trembling.

He stopped drooling.

He looked down at the Bowie knife protruding from his chest, looked forlornly at MaryLou, and said in a weak voice, "My name really is John Smith, you know," before he ever so slowly collapsed onto his face.

MaryLou and Benny said nothing for the longest moment, moved only when they heard a distant but distinct alien bellow down in the valley.

"We gotta take it to them," Benny said, favoring his left leg as he dropped down to pry the strange weapon from Smith's lifeless hands.

"It stands to reason," she agreed, helping him back to his feet and pulling a twig from the hole in his leg. "Those army guys figure this out, they'll be able to blow it to kingdom come." She chortled. "Swiss cheese it to death."

Benny nodded. And smiled. "Then we haul ass back here and set up a stand or something, what do you say?"

MaryLou slapped his back. "Army, you ain't half bad, you know that?"

He blushed.

She laughed.

And after giving the pitiful Smith a hasty but reverent burial, they raced down the mountainside with the only thing on this Earth that could kill the invader.

Artie sat proudly on the palomino as the wooden gate with the barbed wire wrapped around it opened on twice-daily-oiled hinges. The tree stood beside him.

"You know," Artie said, watching the troops gathering behind him, "when the major told me to come get the cavalry, I had no idea."

The tree winked at him. "Don't sweat it, man. Just get going. You guys are the only thing on this Earth that can kill that damned invader."

Casopia had a bad feeling about Hooker's plan.

In the first place, she didn't really know what it was; and in the second place, that *Thing* didn't look as if it had spent a lot of time studying random scripts from *The Gary Moore Show*.

If there was only something she could do.

If only she understood exactly what that dope was up to.

Well, she told herself, you won't find out standing here behind a tree.

Reluctantly she dropped to her hands and knees and crept out of the woods and into the ditch, moving as slowly as she could so as not to disrupt the scientist's concentration or draw unwanted attention to herself.

Her face ran with sweat.

Her palms stung with the scrape of stone and pebble.

She prayed that Nick would not falter or screw up.

Then she saw him plant his hands on his hips, look up into the very face of Death itself, and say, "Hey, big fella, you want to go home now, before you get hurt?"

The *Thing* grumbled.

"You know, this is my lifelong dream, and you don't look so dreamy to me, you big toad."

I knew it, Casopia thought; damn, I knew it.

The *Thing* grunted.

"You have one chance, and then I'm afraid I'm going to have to hurt you."

The *Thing* lanced a casual heat ray at him, but Hooker didn't move, didn't flinch, and the ray scorched the earth not an inch from his shoes.

"Okay, if that's the way you want it."

Casopia held her breath.

Hooker lowered his hands, raised his head to look the *Thing* squarely in whatever was up there in the still thinning smoke, and said in a voice so powerful it rose above the battlefield like a Thanksgiving hymn, "Say goodnight, Gracie!"

There was silence.

There was tension.

Casopia crossed her fingers.

And the *Thing* said, "You're fired, Harry," before seven different rays diced him to death, then fried his little ash.

◆ 4 ◆

Chita slammed on the brakes and browbeat the Dilemma to a sideways halt.

Kent, tangled in the antlers, managed to avoid centrifugal destruction and staggered to his feet on the roof.

And Private Ham Delphim, not six inches from the passenger door, took aim at Kent's royal forehead.

Many members of the crowd, especially the more knowledgeable women, shrieked their dismay; a few of the soldiers muttered rebelliously; Private Fabian Lamanza gallantly pushed Kitty O'Malley behind him and wondered what the hell the sarge would do in a stupid situation like this; and Chita slammed open her door, climbed out, and made sure that Delphim saw the machine gun nestled against her side.

"This," said Kent loudly, "is ridiculous." With an effort that nearly cost him a year or two's growth, he ignored the barrel of the rifle and addressed the officer standing on the tank, whose cannon was also pointed at his head. "You are planning to shoot civilians, sir, when there is a monster right on our tail? Don't you think that's rather backward?"

A heartbeat of tension.

A muffled clearing of someone's throat.

Somewhere off to the left, in the window of an unscathed tailor shop no one had noticed before, the geriatric musical trio struck up a suitable atmospheric selection.

Kent, fed up with just about everything, including the antler that had snared his right sleeve, demanded, "Well?"

The horn player blatted.

"At ease, Private," the major said at last, took off her helmet, and shook out her luxurious raven hair.

"Oh, man," Chita moaned.

For his part, Kent smiled, frowned, smiled again, then frowned when he realized that he had no idea how to react. This development certainly wasn't covered in his father's privately published wartime memoirs. So, tossing away the script with no conscious intention of littering, he leapt nimbly from the car and strode through the barricade of Jeeps to the tank, aware that all eyes were on him, that Chita was right behind him, and that the closer he got, the better the major looked.

"I have vital news," he announced once he had reached the forward tread.

"Perhaps you do, Mr. Montana," the major answered stiffly. "But as you can see, we have everything under control. You may take your place in the crowd now, thank you."

He shook his head. "I don't think you understand the full circumstances of this situation, Major. Miss Juarel here and I have just returned from the utter annihilation of . . . Gander Palace."

"What!" exclaimed Mayor Ellader, shoving his way through the crowd. "All of it?"

"Every stone," Kent informed him regretfully. "There is nothing left but a bloody great hole in the ground."

Consternation blossomed as the word was passed to the rear ranks of the gathered populace. It was shocking. If the Palace had fallen, could anything in the Pond be safe? A few began heated discussions of immediate evacuation plans. Some others wondered aloud about the so-called reinforcements the major had promised them.

Above it all, Kent tried to make himself heard, but the fear became palpable as the voices grew, and it wasn't long before a full-scale panic appeared on the horizon.

"Done good, Lord," Chita muttered at his shoulder.

His smile was brittle, but his following leap onto the tank was impressive, and he was soon face-to-face with something he firmly believed the British Army ought to look into, soon.

"Major," he said, keeping his voice low, "without meaning any disrespect, I really don't think that what you have here is going to stop that thing from destroying this town."

"What did he say?" the mayor demanded.

The major's expression was confident, and a little smug. "It may come as a surprise to you, Mr. Montana, but my men are specially trained for this sort of terrorist behavior. They will do us all proud." She touched his cheek with a battle-hardened yet tender finger. "Besides, I don't need a soap opera butler to tell me my business."

"Daytime drama," he snapped.

"Whatever."

"What did she say?" the mayor pleaded.

Kent glanced toward the burning sky and scowled. "Again, with all due respect, Major, my friend and I are the only civilians in this town now who have had any experience with this thing. I do think we know what we're doing."

"You're not doing anything," she pointed out.

"Well, damnit, we would if you'd give us the chance," he responded tightly. He took her arm, noted the muscle there, noted the sudden not unattractive twitch in her cheek, and gave her his best conspiratorial smile. "Look, I don't want to step on your toes, Major, but I do think you ought to reconsider exiling us to the crowd." He scanned the waiting crowd. "In fact, I doubt they'd let you."

In the air, then, a rhythmic and deep sound, much like a giant strolling through a fairy tale. Everyone immediately looked east.

"We're running out of time, Major."

The major vacillated. "The country. The world. We . . . we must stop it here."

"I know that," he said, mixing kindness with firmness. "All I'm trying to do is avoid a major setback."

"Private!" she screamed. "Shoot this sonofabitch!"

Kent teetered backward when she yanked her arm from his grip, fell to the street when she put a hand to his chest and shoved. Luckily he was able to land on his feet, though not without a bit of athletic twisting, and when he was able to catch his breath, he saw Chita glaring at him.

"Well, why didn't you help me?" he demanded.

"You was doing all right with that lady up there," she said primly. "Didn't want to cramp your style."

The booming grew louder.

Chita leaned on the machine gun. "What did you mean, we're the only ones that have experience with that thing?"

"Well, we do," he said, hating to sound so defensive.

"You think running away is experience?"

"It almost fried us."

She looked extremely doubtful. "Yeah, well, I think they could call us on that one, Lord."

At that moment, Kent had half a mind to forget the whole damn thing and go home. To Scotland. Even his mother was more manageable than this, and her assassins could always be bribed. But when he heard a little girl crying in the crowd, heard a mother attempting to comfort her child, he reared up onto the tank again and grabbed the major's shoulders.

"We *will* work together," he said with teeth clenched. "We can't do it without you, you can't do it without us." He sniffed. "Well, maybe you can, but it won't be fun." He closed one eye. "Is that motor oil you're wearing?"

"You like it?"

He never had time to answer.

Private Fabian Lamanza leapt onto the hood of his Jeep and pointed. "Hey, Major, we got company!"

Kent turned just as a billow of smoke and steam rounded the far bend of the road.

The major sputtered.

Kent whirled to the assembly and shouted, "Get the women and children off the streets! Every man with a gun report—now!—to the major. Everyone else find all the cars and trucks you can and form a barrier one hundred yards from these Jeeps. Pile 'em up if you must, but *make sure that* Thing *doesn't find it easy to get through*!"

As the crowd immediately, and noisily, separated into its component parts, the major hugged him quickly. "Thanks, Montana."

Kent lowered his eyes. "Didn't mean to steal your thunder, Major, but time is of the essence."

She kissed him on both cheeks, retucked her hair beneath her helmet, and ordered *Sergeant* Delphim to deploy his men between the Jeeps and the cars.

"Ma'am?" Delphim said.

"Battlefield promotion, Sergeant," she said with a smile. "You're my main man now."

Kent had no time to appreciate the joy that lit the jug-eared private's eyes. He had places to go, things to do, Chita to mollify, and a mission to stop four earnest soldiers who were trying to muscle the Dilemma down the road to the barricade. When they protested his interference, he told them he hadn't meant *his* car, for god's sake, jumped in, and drove it into the first safe place he could find, which happened to be the newspaper reception room.

Once back on the street, Chita grabbed him, kissed him, and said, "You want to see my breasts?"

The thundering footsteps of the *Thing* grew nearer.

"What?"

Her dark eyes softened. "*Gringo* Baron, we ain't got time for introductions and stuff. Besides, we already know each other."

From O'Malley's office, a gentle violin and a muted horn.

"Anyway, I think maybe I'm losing you to that dumb major broad. I don't think I want to do that."

Kent held her arms and gazed into her eyes. "Chita, this is crazy, you know that."

She pressed into him.

Well, he thought, maybe not quite crazy, but it certainly wasn't the time for it. Although, he had heard that war did funny things to people, and perhaps an interlude of lustful spring before the coming dread of Martian winter might be just the thing to recharge his batteries while he figured out how in the bloody hell he'd gotten into this in the first place.

A shattering of glass distracted him.

Chita said, "Nuts," and they watched as dozens of automobiles both new and old converged at a spot where a scrawny, ducktailed private stood. With sharp gestures and limber veronicas born of dodging pursuit police cruisers, the soldier orchestrated the preventive demolition derby with a skill that soon had his fellows hooting and cheering.

Then a frazzled, rumpled man came up and said, "You're Kent Montana."

"That's right."

The man flashed a yellowed card. "O'Malley. Press. Gander Pond. I want to know if you made contact with that alien thing yet, and if so, were you able to ascertain its precise mission here on Earth?"

A tree blew up in front of the mayor's real estate office.

"That answer your question?" Kent said wryly.

"Say goodnight, Gracie?" Casopia screamed at the pile of pale drifting ash in the middle of the highway. "Are you out of your goddamned mind? Say goodnight, Gracie?"

Angrily she kicked at the remains of Nicodemus Hooker's lifelong dream, then gasped at her callousness and fell at once to her knees. "God, I'm sorry, you idiot," she sobbed, and scooped as much of the ash as she could into her palm. When she realized she had nothing to carry him home in, yet reluctant to leave him behind to the mercy of the uncaring winds, she did the first thing she could think of—she shoved him down her neckline, muttered a secular prayer as she dusted her hands, and stood up to watch the back of the *Thing* as it lumbered toward Gander Pond.

"You know the guy?"

She yelped, spun, had a fist cocked and ready, before she recognized the somewhat unclean uniform of the United States Army. On the other hand, the little guy in it was cute in an earthy Mediterranean way, not exactly her type, and Jesus, girl, are you out of your goddamn mind?

"Yes," she answered shakily. "Yes, I did."

Milos Athnos jabbed a fist toward the monster. "That thing killed my best friend."

"I'm sorry."

"Not as sorry as that sonofabitch is going to be when I get through with it."

Right, Casopia thought. Damn right.

"We have to get to town," she said, grabbing the corporal's arm and dragging him toward the ruins of the Palace. "I have, or I think I have, the way to destroy that thing." She started to run. "That's what my . . . friend was doing."

"Well," Milos said, stuffing grenades into his pockets, "he didn't do it right, did he? No offense."

"As best he could," she said, more to herself than to the grizzled corporal. "As best he could."

And as soon as she found Kent, she would tell him Hooker's idea, and between them, she knew, she just *knew*, they would be victorious where poor old Nick had failed.

"Hey, lady," the soldier protested when they reached the other shoulder, "that ain't the way to town."

She smiled without humor over her shoulder. "My friend, in my business, you learn very quickly that shortcuts can be a lifesaver."

The soldier seemed confused.

"Don't worry about it," she said. "It's a long story."

"Maybe you can tell me over a drink sometime."

This time her smile was rueful. "If there is a sometime, soldier boy."

Milos nodded wisely. Then: "Hey, you gonna tell me what this secret weapon is?"

"On the way," she promised. "On the way."

And together they vanished into the fire and the smoke.

"Wow, Sparky!" Janis said. "Look at that!"

Sparky hunkered down and growled low in his throat.

The little girl stood on the last corner in town, not one hundred and thirty-two yards from the bend in the road. And there, just ahead, was the neatest, prettiest cloud of smoke she had ever seen in her entire life.

The earth trembled as footsteps approached.

"Wow, Sparky, maybe we can have a new friend, huh?" She knelt beside the dog and hugged it. It wagged its tail. She kissed it, scratched it between its ears, and said, "Well, I guess we better be going."

Sparky barked.

And Janis Ellader stepped into the road.

"This?" Benny exclaimed. "We're using this?"

MaryLou glowered at him as she reset her beret. "What's the matter with this? You think I got a limo or something I keep at my place for emergencies? Jesus, Hart, I thought you was an army, not a wimp."

Benny sighed in resignation. He limped out of the trees onto the road and sighed again. Behind him, MaryLou wrestled a bicycle built for two out of its hiding place. He watched her, looked up the highway, and decided he was too weary to sigh a third time. Besides, the little rainbow pills she had given him were beginning to wear off, and the hole in his leg had begun a deep-seated throbbing.

"Don't know if I can do it," he said when she hopped onto the rear seat and motioned him into the pilot's position. He pointed to his leg.

"Don't sweat it, army," she answered brusquely. "All you have to do is steer, maybe give me a hand with the good leg, and I'll do the rest."

He supposed it would be petty to argue. After all, saving the unliberated United States of America was his idea, and backing out now probably wouldn't look too good in his official biography.

"Move it!" she snapped as she strapped the weapon onto the brace bar between them. "C'mon, boy, we're losing time!"

"All right, all right," he muttered.

Gingerly, holding his breath against possible onslaughts of pain, he straddled the fleece-covered seat and took hold of the handlebars. Then he put his left foot on the left pedal and stuck his right leg straight ahead, out of harm's way. If he got too tired, he could always coast.

"You okay?"

He nodded.

And he fought to keep himself from closing his eyes as the ungainly vehicle wobbled forward. Slowly. A little less slowly. A tilt to the right, a quick swerve to the left, compensate, oversteer, keep away from the chuckholes, and for god's sake don't hit a tree. So much to think about, so little time.

Almost before he knew it, however, they were rolling at speed, the wind whistling gaily through the hole in his leg, and all his attention was focused on the vivid and disturbing scene of battle and defeat that unrolled as they passed— overturned and burning Jeeps, bodies, empty ammunition clips, spots and blots and veritable puddles of blood. A white limousine with four flat tires.

"Damn," MaryLou said over the wind they made. "Ain't this something?"

It was.

It was also a pause for serious thought about what they

were getting into so fast now that his eyes had started to water. How the hell big was this thing anyway? How strong was it? What kind of weapons did it have that it could afford to leave behind a ray gun of such incredible power?

He steered around a hissing raccoon.

"You know," he called over his shoulder, "maybe we ought to find a back way or something."

"You chickening out, army?"

"No! I just don't want to run up its back, that's all."

Pockets of smoke lying close to the ground.

A lone tire straddling the white line.

A cop without a head.

A cowboy without a head.

"You know any back roads?" MaryLou asked.

"No," he answered sadly.

"Then I guess," she said phlegmatically, "we ain't got much choice."

Oh, I wouldn't know about that, he thought dourly, but he kept such treason to himself. Not only was his back to her, and thus a perfect target for that monster knife and her unerring aim, but also his conscience had burped again, which was getting to be a pain, and for some damned reason he couldn't see himself running away with the one thing that would stop this unimaginable invasion in its tracks.

He missed the front half of a Jeep by inches.

Hell. He hated having a conscience.

"Hang in there, army. Hang in there, you're doing good."

Right. And maybe, when this thing was over, he could have an operation or something.

Artie Chong leaned low over the palomino's neck, urging it onward, onward, ever onward, with his face buried in its mane and the tails of his frock coat flapping in the wind. There was nothing on this profitable earth that would make him look in the direction they were heading or the direction from which they had just come. Things moved too fast, and too close, for his Oriental comfort. He didn't even bother to attempt to guide it; the animal seemed to know, again, exactly where to go, what turns to make. Which was all right with him because he was still trying to figure out how the army had fit all those other horses into that hole in the ground from which they had emerged, riders and all, once the tree had made its report.

Sophia wasn't going to believe it.

Sordette, on the other hand, would probably want to know all the fascinating details.

The horse snorted.

Artie Chong agreed. One of these days, hopefully when he was at least ninety, his animal magnetism was going to get him in serious trouble.

A huge black stallion drew even with him.

"Chong!" its rider called.

Artie turned his face without opening his eyes.

"How much farther?"

"Ask the horse," he called back.

They rode on. Through the dark.

"I did," the rider finally answered. "He said to ask you."

Artie hated Occidental jokes. They never made sense; and even when they did, they never made sense. His response, then, was an inscrutable shrug, a wag of an eyebrow, and a tacit promise that they would reach their destination long before anyone really wanted to.

It was a moment of sublime terror and supreme confidence, something not felt so strongly or so giddily since Kent had discovered the time bomb in the shoe box under his bed and had successfully dusted it for his mother's fingerprints. Then, as now, he didn't know whether to laugh or cry; then, he had rowed into the North Sea on the yacht his mother had stolen the engines from and dropped the bomb overboard; now, he didn't have the faintest idea what to do.

He stood on the tank. On his left was the barrel of its cannon and on the side was Major Settbach. On his right, Chita waited with her machine gun, heroic in the wind that blew back her hair and ruffled the headband she had found in a nearly looted ladies' clothing store. It ruffled because it was a forty-dollar silk garter. When he rather tactlessly pointed that out to her, she had wanted to know, altogether too sweetly for his taste, if he wanted to make something of it. He hadn't. One alien fight was enough for one night, thank you very much and where the hell was the cavalry?

Below him, the Jeeps had been redistributed and relined,

and the soldiers stood and knelt tensely behind and beside them. Grenade launchers, rocket launchers, machine guns, rifles, handguns, grenades, bayonets, and all other manner of esoteric weaponry were trained on the smoke cloud that had paused briefly up the road.

Above him left and right were more soldiers, and many of the men of Gander Pond, scattered along on the rooftops and as heavily armed as they were going to get on such short notice. Their expressions and postures were determined; their demeanors stouthearted—after all, this was *their* town, *their* home, and they was proud to be a part of it.

Behind him many of the women who had refused to evacuate were loading extra weapons, preparing bandages and splints, and, back by the hotels, setting up a field hospital under the direction of Sophia Chong, who sent a runner up every five minutes, wanting to know if anyone had had word about her Artie.

That saddened him, for he knew that many families were going to be rent and torn asunder this day, and only a miracle would prevent it.

Nothing moved.

The still night broken only by the jangling of a rifle strap, a muffled cough, the scrape of a boot.

A woman hurried boldly to the tank and called his name softly. He turned as Chita said, "God, another one?" and looked into the eyes of someone he knew he didn't know but felt as if he did. She was not slender, nor was she overweight; she wore farm clothes, had straggly hair, and when she spat tobacco onto the street, the act seemed not all unladylike.

"Bitinia," she said, pointing to her chest.

He waited.

"You was with my brother when he died."

"The cowboy," Chita reminded him, and drew a finger across her neck.

Kent glared at her tactlessness, then nodded to the woman. "I was, yes. A brave man."

"Ex always was," she said. "Anyways, I just want you to know I appreciate it."

He didn't understand, but he nodded anyway.

She spat again. "So where the hell's my horse?"

"On a secret mission," the major interjected before he could respond. "Now please, get back where you belong."

Bitinia Player scowled at her, scowled at Kent, then spat on the tank and strode off, dragging a bazooka behind her.

Americans, Kent thought, and reached into his jeans pocket, pulled out something he fingered for a moment, and affixed it to his shirt collar without taking his eyes off the invisible dark figure at the end of the road.

"What's that?" Chita whispered.

"St. Andrew's cross," he said. "He's the patron saint of my country."

"For luck?"

He nodded.

She reached over and touched it reverently. "Emeralds and gold. Very nice. Where'd you get it?"

"My mother gave it to me the day I left for America."

"Ah."

"It was poisoned at the time."

Her hand snapped back.

"It's all right. I put a new pin on it."

Someone coughed.

A runner whispered a question to the major, who scowled and said, "No, he's not back yet. You think I'd be standing up here if he was?"

A rifle bolt was thrown and a round placed into a chamber.

Kent leaned over the barrel and said, "Pardon me, Major, but I just had a thought."

The major looked at him and bit her lower lip.

Kent was grateful for wartime tolerance between reluctant allies. "All that activity before, when the *Thing* first came off the mountain and you arrived? All those helicopters and such? Why haven't they returned? Why didn't the army send you more men?"

"Sorry, Mr. Montana—"

"Baron," Chita corrected. "This here's a baron."

The major's eyes widened only slightly when Kent nodded modestly. "Well, your lordship," she continued, "the fact is, we're sealed off."

"Sealed . . . off?"

"That's correct. A preventive measure. Nothing in, nothing out."

"But we could use the help."

"Exactly why I am here."

Kent stared at her troopers, stared at the townspeople, stared at Chita. Who lifted a shoulder.

He swallowed. "And what," he asked flatly, "will happen if we don't stop that *Thing* here?" He laughed dryly. "They going to drop an atom bomb on it?"

Chita jabbed him with an elbow.

The major looked straight ahead and said, "That's classified, Mr. Mon—your lordship."

Taking a few precious seconds from the probable end of his life, Kent organized his thoughts, then kicked them all to hell. "Major, you will excuse me, but if we are not successful, top secret isn't going to mean a hell of a lot."

Major Settbach refused to look at him. "I'm sorry. That's all I can tell you."

"Shit," said Chita, "they're gonna ace us."

Kent inhaled slowly and deeply. "And I suppose," he said with undisguised rancor, "that there's a timetable for this . . . top secret?"

Then the major turned her head. "Dawn." And looked back at her men.

He looked at Chita.

She shrugged and said, "It's traditional."

His response, such as it might have been and most likely not in English, was forestalled by a woman's hysterical scream. He whirled in time to see Eunice Ellader break from the compassionate grip of a fellow conscripted nurse and run toward the line of Jeeps.

"Stop her!" Settbach yelled.

Eunice bowled over a grasping Horace O'Malley, dodged Ham Delphim's desperate lunge, and screamed again. "My baby! My baby! My god, someone save my baby!"

"What she talking about?" Chita asked as the woman was finally tackled by four privates.

Kent didn't know.

Not until he happened to look up just as Private Fabian Lamanza shouted, "Oh my god! *Look!*"

Kent gasped, Chita moaned, and the major took off her helmet and slammed it onto the gun barrel.

There, skipping out of the dark on the left side of the street, was a small girl and her dog.

She headed straight for the cloud.

And she was too far away for anyone to stop her.

–IV–

Last Reel,
and Testament

◆ 1 ◆

IT couldn't remember when IT had last had such an enjoyable time. It almost made up for the loss of the ship, the loss of the food supply, and the reasonably assumed loss of the eggs IT had been transporting to the greenhouse nursery on Jupiter.

So much killing and destruction fairly made ITs blood boil with ecstasy.

And there was so much to learn from these curious bipedal idiots who persisted in attempting to destroy IT.

It was to laugh.

So IT did.

Puny weapons, puny bipeds, puny appeals to religion and natural selection—the only scare IT suffered had come at the hands of the curiously colored creature that evidently had discovered the methods of ITs training. IT was so astonished, IT had nearly given the game away.

But IT had persevered.

It had fried the biped before it was able to complete the sequence.

And in so being unnerved, IT decided there would be no more mister nice guy.

Death.

Destruction.

Doom.

So ITs course was charted, ITs destiny unthwarted when one of the bipeds' young ones broke from the shadows and stood in front of IT, with an annoying little sub-creature prancing beside it. Though the little thing distantly reminded IT of the sorrowful loss of a generation of ITs, back there atop that mountain, IT paused only a second before leaning out of ITs clever cloud cover and saying, ''Hey, kids, what time is it?''

· 2 ·

It was, to Kent, one of those macabre moments forever frozen in time: the U.S. Army's best immobile with shock and disbelief; Mrs. Ellader immobile with fear and terror in the arms of her photo-taking husband; the townspeople immobile with horror and morbid fascination; he, Chita, and the major, immobile with helplessness and shock.

Heavy breathing.

The dog's distant yapping.

Something foul and furry-feathered reaching inexorably out of the smoke.

But when a much too vivid image of the Jersey cowboy's decapitation flashed through his mind, Kent shook off his stupor and asked himself, rather bluntly, if he was going to be a goddamned bloody butler for the rest of his life.

The answer was obvious.

Nevertheless, he sprang from the top of the tank, sprinted through a gap in the Jeeps, and brought his rifle to bear as he rounded the barrier heap of automobiles.

But he knew he would be too late.

The little girl backed away as she shook her pigtailed head.

The dog rushed in front of her for loyal, dim-witted protection.

He ran on in spite of the odds.

The *Thing* grumbled greedily.

Suddenly, from out of a side street and nearly running him down without so much as a *watch where you're going*, sped what he recognized as a beautifully preserved, perfectly tuned, lemon-yellow '34 Cord convertible. An elderly, sombrero-attired woman drove, a portly old man with a horn cringed in the back while another one slept with a violin cradled in his arms, and standing in the passenger seat was a man a few years younger than he, slender, of modest appearance, and wearing a cloth tape measure around his neck.

The agile Cord darted deftly between the child and the *Thing*, and the standing man courageously, if a little foolhardily, swooped both little girl and little dog into his arms, just as the furry-hairy appendage slashed lethally through the space where child and creature had stood.

Kent stopped.

Cheers erupted behind him.

The Cord bumped over the curb as it turned and swung back toward him. Nimbly he stepped out of the way when it braked beside him and the man gently deposited the little ones safely on the pavement.

"You be careful now," he said to the child.

Kent shook his head in admiration. "That was terribly brave of you," he said.

"Nothing to it," the man replied modestly. He turned to the old woman. "Alice, the next time I go on one of your vacations, shoot me first. Now get me the hell out of here. And don't you dare—"

But the old woman had already plucked from her sombrero one of the larger grapes, which Kent's eye for detail noted had been cleverly filed into a razor-sharp missile, and had pitched it toward the cloud.

The *Thing* inside bellowed in anger.

"Shit," the man said.

"You'd better go on," Kent told him. "Mr. . . ."

"Blackthorne," said the man, to a thunderous burst of applause from the townsfolk. He waved, nodded, and was thrown into his seat when Alice slammed the car into gear and vanished in a stream of exhaust.

Janis cried, "Oh, please, come back, come back!"

At that moment, her mother rushed up, grabbed the child into her arms, and rushed away, sobbing.

The *Thing* began to move.

Its footsteps sounded like someone thumping a massive ceremonial drum, its breathing resembled a locomotive coming up to steam, and the death rays that ignited the houses it passed looked exactly like death rays setting horrendous and unquenchable conflagrations.

Kent ran back toward the tank, ice cubes of fear rolling about in his stomach. Nothing was going to defeat that beastly alien, and unless he uncovered a handy streak of cowardice damned soon, his mother was at last going to get her wish.

Then the tank fired.

And the soldiers fired.

And the snipers on the rooftops fired.

And Kent was grabbed by Horace O'Malley, who shouted over the din, "Who was that man?"

"I don't know," Kent lied, and pushed him away.

O'Malley scowled, flinched when the tank belched another shell, and darted to the north side of the street, where he found his daughter loading clips for the rifle of a young trooper who looked as if he'd be more at home mugging old ladies and social workers.

"Daddy!" she cried when he dropped to her side.

Puffing, red-faced, he gave her a quick hug before whipping out his charcoal and scrap of paper. "Any news?"

"Oh, Daddy, not now! Can't you see what's happening here?"

He rose slightly, dropped quickly. "Sure. Our house just blew up." He grabbed her hand and squeezed it. "Darlin', you're not mad that I never remarried, are you, and denied you the chance to have a mother in your teen years?"

Her eyes misted over.

"And you're not mad that I never took that job with the *Plain-Dealer*, are you?"

Lips quivering, she shook her head.

"I love you, you know," he said gruffly. "I don't tell you that often enough, I suppose, but I do love you. After all, you're all I have left in this world."

Kitty O'Malley bawled.

Horace duck-walked over to the greasy soldier who'd been watching the scene with narrowed eyes, and gripped the young man's arm. Hard. "Son, you watch after my little girl, you hear? Things get too hot, you get her the hell away, or I'll come for you. I swear I will.''

The private seemed impressed. ''Got it, sir.''

O'Malley nodded solemnly, blew a kiss at his daughter, and made his way back toward what was left of the center of town, his shoulders hunched against the vicious fighting behind him. A navy-blue beam skewed overhead and, as he threw himself to his right, separated the movie theater from its marquee. Smoke and dust enveloped him, choked him, and he didn't resist when strong hands dragged him to safety into the Pagoda.

''Drink this.''

A tin cup of tepid water was placed against his lips, and he took a sip, spat it out, and drank the rest. ''Thanks,'' he managed when he finished.

The fire truck slammed to a halt in front of the theater.

An emerald-green ray blew it up.

''I think we'd better get out of here,'' said a husky female voice.

O'Malley agreed and allowed himself to be led back through the ruins of the dining room into the kitchen, which, all things considered, wasn't in bad shape. Here he saw his rescuer for the first time, and he wondered if he had actually been killed in that last explosion, gone to heaven, and was given recompense for his years of devotion to the memory of his dead wife.

''I know you,'' he said to the incongruously scantily clad woman. ''You're the apprentice chef hereabouts.''

''Yes,'' she acknowledged, dusting off his grimy jacket. ''And I think we're going to die, don't you?''

Another explosion outside. The walls trembled. Plaster fell from the ceiling. An inhuman cry carried over the town.

O'Malley wasn't stupid. He'd seen enough movies to know what this woman meant. He just hoped Kitty would understand in case the building collapsed and crushed them *in flagrante*. He wouldn't care, of course, but he figured he was too old to give a damn about what people said at his funeral.

''Where?'' he asked.

She pointed at the wok table. ''There.''

''There?''

''I'm sorry. It's short notice.''

He kissed her.

She kissed him back.

He kissed her again and was about to go for the gold when the back door crashed in.

Sordette Biletto shrieked and ran trippingly into the night, shoving aside a nun who stood on the threshold with a baseball bat in her hand.

"So," the nun said.

O'Malley puffed his cheeks in indignation. "What the hell do you want?"

"You," she said, and stepped inside, raised the bat to her shoulder, and turned him around roughly. "Outside, newsman."

"What?" He resisted. "You're crazy!"

"Not really," another voice answered, one he recognized as belonging to the Reverend Phyllis Lager. "You have influence in this community, Mr. O'Malley. You have the power of the press behind you. You will go out there and tell them to stop the shooting."

O'Malley whirled in stunned protest, and Phyllis feared he would slug Sister Lillian. The nun's reflexes were quicker, however; she planted the bat squarely in his midsection, returned him as he gasped for a breath, and shoved him out of the kitchen, promising all manner of divine and secular retribution if he didn't do what the Sisters of the Alien Tabernacle Today Society ordered.

Phyllis followed more slowly. She wasn't at all happy with the name the nun had devised on their way here. Nor was she pleased with the nun's assertive personality. One did not win converts by force, but by love, gentle persuasion, and a healthy but subtle dose of Old Testament terror.

She had to admit, however, that in this case, the bat worked.

O'Malley staggered through the window to the pavement, held up his hands in submission, and swore on everything he held dear in the United States Constitution that he would do as Sister Lillian commanded.

"God bless you," the nun responded sincerely.

"Right," the editor said, and looked plaintively at Phyllis, who extended him a comforting theological gesture, then leapt backward into the Pagoda with a terrified squeal when a vicious stream of scarlet heat pulses boiled the blacktop, refried the fire engine, and neatly severed Sister Lillian's wimple from her head.

"Christ!" the editor screamed, and ran like hell.

Phyllis cowered. Whimpered. Covered her ears against the screams and shouts and gunfire and cannonfire and explosions and sirens.

"Phil," she whispered.

Footsteps boomed.

A man raced by, calling upon God to spare them this judgment.

Three women hustled up, rolled the nun onto a stretcher, and raced away, calling upon God to spare them this divine verdict.

The *Thing* roared in agony.

And Phyllis, huddling and trembling there in the semi-dark, realized that she had been spared for, as Phil would have had it, a Purpose. What else could it be? And as such, it was most clearly a circumstance too prophetic to pass up. She smiled. She sprang to her feet. She leapt clumsily from the Pagoda and sprinted across the street, angled to her right toward the far corner, and grabbed onto a lamppost when a fuchsia pulse ray beam took out the rest of the restaurant.

She was right.

It was a Sign.

And she had two martyrs to prove it.

She glanced up Main and saw the undulating tower of steam and smoke inexorably advance upon the defenders' position. Gunfire spat into it, light streaks popped out of it. It was thunder and lightning and all kinds of noise; it was Hell on wheels or whatever the *Thing* used to get from here to there; it was going to be damned difficult to render its vision in four-color neon so that parishioners wouldn't run screaming from the Tabernacle into someplace silly, like a church.

But if that was her task, then so be it.

His Will be done.

The neon would take care of itself.

A beam sheared off the top of the lamppost.

Phyllis tumbled several feet into the side street, landed on her back, and saw stars, heavenly hosts, and a woman in a shredded red dress holding out her hand.

"Let me help you," said the woman.

Phyllis cringed and batted at the hand. "Keep away! Keep away! I am anointed, you jerk, and I must prepare the Tabernacle for the service!"

"She's hysterical," the woman said to a shadowy figure that came up beside her.

"She's nuts," a masculine voice pronounced in disgust.

Oh Lord, Phyllis thought, it's the grubby little man with the interesting but disgusting hands.

She scuttled back until she reached a battered wall, shaking her head but unable to resist when Milos Athnos grabbed her arms and hauled her to her feet.

"I spotted a field hospital down there," he told Casopia. "Maybe we ought to take her there. Shock, I'll bet."

"No!" Phyllis shrieked.

"It's okay," Casopia soothed. "Don't worry. We're going to kill it, and you'll be all right."

Phyllis decked her.

Milos thumped Phyllis.

Casopia looked up from the ground and said, "You take her. I've got to see Kent."

The corporal was not happy, but neither could his latent fear of God permit him to leave a reverend unconscious in the street while all hell broke loose around her. "Okay. Just don't do anything until I get back. I got a score to settle with that thing, y'know."

Casopia nodded, made sure he was truly on his way, then scurried along the devastation that was Main Street, her gaze on the figure of a man standing atop the tank that continued to pour a deadly stream of death into the smoke cloud that had finally reached the first line of defense. He pointed, gestured, occasionally fired a rifle, ducked when a dot of heat ray swept over his head and exploded not ten feet from where Casopia ran. She ducked, weaved, shouted encouragement to those who were reloading, bandaging, helping the wounded, bringing water; she tripped and fell; she lunged to her feet and ran again; she leapt a small crater; angrily she shook off a man who demanded to know what she was feeling at this moment; determinedly she knocked aside an idiot trying to take her picture; furiously she clawed over a pile of bricks and crumbled stone and finally fell gasping against the rear tread of the tank.

The cannon fired.

The tank recoiled.

Casopia was thrown backward just as she shouted, "Kent! Kent, I've got the answer!"

"So tell me," he said, wiping sweat from his brow and slapping another clip into his rifle.

"Tell you what?" Chita asked. Her machine gun had depleted all her ammunition, reducing her to snatching grenades from passing soldiers. Her aim wasn't very good, but it kept the *Thing* guessing.

"The answer."

"What answer?"

He stared at her. "Look, you said you had the answer. All I want to know is, what's the answer?"

"What's the question?"

Horror swept his emotions, his limbs, his mind. This woman had been sent by his mother! There was no other reasonable explanation for her existence. She had been dispatched to these shores to reduce, befuddle, and weaken him. She was, in other words, an assassin.

"Damn," he said.

Chita patted his cheek. "Don't worry about it, Lord. It's the heat of battle and all that."

A lull in the fighting followed her words, and the major abandoned the tank to circulate among her men, urging them to stand fast, to reload, to aim for the good parts and stop shooting the cars. Kent, meanwhile, dropped into a sitting position and faced west, nostrils wrinkling at the stench of fighting, ears stuffed with the roar of the cannon, head pounding and arms aching and, "Hey, Chita, isn't that Casopia down there?"

Chita immediately flew to the ground and knelt beside the fallen woman. Kent watched them—Chita solicitous and caring, the hooker bedraggled, nearly naked, and insistent upon something.

"Hey, Baron," Chita called up to him. "She says she has the answer."

Two of them, he thought; my lord, Mother, how resourceful can you be?

He smiled gamely.

"No kidding, Baron, I think you'd better listen to her."

Of course. Why not?

Moving stiffly, he made an *I'll be back* gesture to the major, dropped to the ground, rubbed his arms and back, and stared dumbly when Chita helped Casopia to her feet, and the two of them stared dumbly at him in turn.

"You got a problem?" Chita asked.

"Kent," Casopia said, trying to hold up her neckline with one hand and brush her hair from her eyes with the other, "Nick knows how to kill the monster."

Kent nodded. "Oh?"

"Yes, and he died testing his theory!"

"The guy's dead?" Chita asked.

Casopia nodded mournfully.

"Aw nuts."

Kent scrubbed his face hard with his palms. Had he heard correctly? Was that ill-dressed but well-meaning scientist, the only hope anyone here had for salvation, dead? Gone? Leaving him and Gander Pond to Major Settbach and her soldiers? Dead? Their last hope? Gone? Forever?

Chita slapped him.

He snared her wrist and scowled. "What the hell was that for?"

"You were dazed," she said concernedly.

"I was not. I was thinking."

"You think you were thinking, but you were dazed." She looked to Casopia, who nodded. "Battle fatigue, something like that. You're trying too hard to do everything, you know what I mean? You should rest or something."

Her compassion was genuine. He knew that. He'd been an actor too long not to know acting when he saw it.

"Chita," he said, "do you know my mother?"

She looked around. "Why? She here?"

He hugged her. He kissed her. He looked over her shoulder and said, "I'm sorry about Nick," to Casopia.

"It's all right. He was a jerk, but he gave me the secret before he died." A tear skidded through the soot and dirt on her face. "He died for me, Kent. Can you imagine it? A jerk in a lavender jacket died for me."

She broke down, and Chita gathered her into the embrace she shared with Kent. The three of them, then, stood there as the *Thing* reopened its campaign by kicking the heap of cars all to hell and scrap.

And when the major came behind the tank and saw them, he said, ''Stick around, Major, I think we've got the answer.''

· 3 ·

They had stopped shooting, and IT was worried.

Things, excluding ITself, weren't right.

Until this moment, IT had not even begun to include in ITs calculations the possibility, however remote, that IT had been drawn into a clever trap the insidious likes of which IT had not encountered since the year IT had done a little free-lance paramecia stomping on the far side of the eleventh planet of the fourth star in a galaxy IT had never heard of, but the pay was good so IT didn't really mind.

But there had been that stupid trap.

As a consequence, IT had nearly flooded the canal during that attention-getting enterprise, and wariness had been ITs hallmark ever since.

The trouble was, as IT finally saw it through all the swarming murk and self-produced atmospheric pollution that served as a screen for ITs multi-beamed attack, IT had been having too good a time.

IT was enjoying ITself.

Now, in and of itself and all the circumstances of ITs appearance here, that wasn't a bad thing. Not to take some delight in one's mission, programmed or not, was bound to lead ultimately to misfortune and, perhaps, even permanent termination of the life form most dear to IT.

On the other hand, to exhibit too much glee, too much abandon, too much sheer personal gratification during ITs prime invasion function, might lead to inattention and, therefore, to carelessness.

As in this case.

Maybe.

There they were, all those ludicrous little bipeds hiding behind those curious vehicles, and they weren't doing anything at all. They weren't trying to kill IT, they weren't trying to contact IT, they hadn't even made a preliminary move to worship IT. What kind of way was that to fend off an interstellar encroachment?

Ponderously and perplexedly IT stepped back several yards and swiveled ITs cranium until IT could see back the way IT had come.

Could that other biped, the one so clearly ranking in intelligence far above the others, have somehow communicated its horrifying and potentially lethal discovery to these other bipeds?

Impossible.

That would require an advanced telepathic function none of ITs sophisticated scanning devices had been able to detect. Unless, of course such an advanced function included the equally advanced ability to block all those scanning devices. Which his devices were equipped to detect anyway, so it didn't matter whether they had the ability to block the ability or not.

Which meant they didn't have it.

Which meant IT had eradicated the only true threat to ITs continuation, other than the headache all those shells were giving IT.

So why weren't they fighting?

Well, IT decided smugly as IT switched ITs concentration back to the destructive matter at hand, since I'm just the cleverest fellow 'twas ever my fortune to know, I'll just have to figure it out.

Why is it standing so still, Benny wondered apprehensively. Why doesn't it try to fry us, or stomp us, or slice us to bloody ribbons?

He looked over his shoulder apprehensively, but MaryLou only glared at him and signaled him to keep on pedaling, for god's sake, let's take advantage of the situation.

As best he could with one leg, he pedaled.

He prayed.

He practically stripped his lips of skin nibbling at them in his anxiety.

And he tried not to look to his left as he steered the bicycle built for two around the camouflage of smoke and steam and other floating stuff that surrounded the *Thing* he had never really gotten a good look at since the invasion had begun, and didn't really want to get a good look at now.

If he did, it would mean that the *Thing* would be able to get a good look at him.

And if it got a good look at him, then the liberation army was going to be flatter than cow flop in a race across a pasture.

He heard MaryLou puffing with exertion.

He heard the creature breathing thoughtfully.

He nearly cheered when he saw the ragged but stout line of defense looming ahead of him—tank, cars, Jeeps, soldiers, civilians, houses burning down around their foundations, stores crushed into so much molten glass and aluminum, gaping craters in the blacktop, the distant weep and wail of the injured and the dying.

He blinked.

He veered sharply around the tangled heap of automobiles and pickups, some of which had been, to his trained eye, kicked all to hell and scrap, and headed directly for the tank, since, he figured, that's where the officer in charge must have his command post. Only Captain Kirk had been dumb enough to go down in the trenches with the privates, and everybody knows what happened to him.

"Halt!"

MaryLou and Benny both slammed on the brakes.

A faint rumbling, much like thunder, filled the silence between the squeal and the stop.

A private stepped around a Jeep and aimed a rifle at them. "Who goes there?"

"The monster from outer space," MaryLou growled.

"Fire!" the private shouted.

"Asshole!" a grease-haired private snapped as he slapped the first private's rifle to one side and Benny relaxed the grip his innards had on his bowels. "Jesus, Ham, they aren't the creature, for crying out loud."

"Well, they said they were," Delphim pouted.

"Sure. And if I say I'm General Electric, you gonna believe that too?"

Delphim sneered. "You only been in five years, same as me, you dummy. You can't be a general. But them, they said—"

"Hey, shrimp, you blind or what?" MaryLou snarled at him. She cocked her pheasant feather beret and squinted menacingly until Delphim gave her a satisfactory hint of cowering. Then she said, "Who the hell is your commanding officer?" She grabbed the weapon from its place on the bike and held it up. "We got the thing that's gonna fry that thing."

"Yeah, right," said Fabian Lamanza.

"She's telling the truth," Benny insisted. "That's a weapon we found at the spaceship."

Lamanza giggled. "Spaceship? Jesus. Ham, these people think they were on a spaceship." He laughed.

Field Commission Sergeant Ham Delphim disdainfully shoved the private against a Jeep. "And where do you think the critter came from, huh?" He shoved him again. "How do you think it got here, huh?" He shoved him again. "What do you think crashed up there, huh?"

Lamanza ducked the next shove and held his rifle up protectively. "All right, all right, already. God." He looked at Benny. "So. You were in a spaceship."

Benny nodded.

The thunder grew louder.

Lamanza couldn't help another giggle. "What was it, shaped like a flying saucer?"

"No. A '59 Caddy."

Delphim laughed. "See? What did I tell you, you jerk?" He pointed at the tank, his bearing erect, his voice a study in military efficiency. "Major Settbach's right over there. You'd better get going. We're in a quiet moment now, but who knows how long it will last?"

Benny nodded, MaryLou started pedaling, and as they passed between the two soldiers, he heard the jug-eared one say, "Christ, the next thing you know, Fabian, you'll be saying all that thunder is horses or something."

• • •

Ah, the hell with it, IT thought.

IT drew ITself up to full height, lit the skies with errant pulses and ray and sparkling beams, and with a great bellow and a greater roar and a curiously high-pitched challenge that might have resembled "Yo, Rinty!" IT charged.

◆ 4 ◆

When Kent Montana last witnessed a council of war, it was when the leading lady of *Passions and Power* plotted with her two cousins and best friend to murder the bastard son of her fourth or fifth husband in order to place the blame and a jail sentence on her current lover, because her current lover was currently having an affair with her daughter by her second husband, the one who had disappeared in Albania during a training exercise with the CIA.

This one, however, was ridiculous.

It took place in the middle of the intersection marked by Gander Pond's four depleted hotels. The major had suggested this particularly vulnerable spot in case they were overheard, but refused, upon questioning, to say by whom.

Far up Main Street, Fabian Lamanza, newly appointed sergeant, valiantly held the line against the lumbering charge of the *Thing*, which, it was estimated, would reach the tank sometime before dawn at its current rate of attack. The field hospital had been evacuated. Most of the downtown was deserted now, save for the army and the snipers.

The sky began to lighten in the east.

"You gotta be kidding," said Major Settbach scornfully. "Say goodnight, Gracie?" She actually snorted derision. "Lady, we haven't got time for games here. That *Thing* is going to barbecue this town in about half an hour."

"Who's Gracie?" asked a bewildered Sergeant Ham Delphim.

Casopia appealed silently to Kent for support.

He looked at her, at the major, at the sergeant, at Benny Hart, at the woman dressed in black, at Chita, at Milos Athnos, and then down the street whence came the sound of one hell of a thunderstorm. "She may be right, Major," he allowed at last. "It has occurred to me that this creature has been muttering to itself on occasion."

The major scoffed.

"And may I remind you that Dr. Hooker was, after all, a respected scientist?"

The major, the sergeant, and the corporal exchanged barely tolerant looks that told them all quite plainly what the military thought of civilian scientists. Especially those who field-tested their theories without years of Pentagon research and congressional hearings.

Unfortunately Athnos proceeded to ruin the moment by saying, "Wait a minute, wait a minute. Excuse me, Major, but you know, just before that sucker fried that guy—sorry, lady—I did hear something." He scratched his grubby cheeks. "At the time I figured I was hearing things, being so caught up in avenging the sarge's death and all."

"Now honestly, Corporal," the major said impatiently.

"Sir," said Ham Delphim, "who's Gracie?"

"Excuse me," Benny interrupted, "but even it that's true, it doesn't matter, right? I mean, we got the thing's gun anyway, so what difference does it make? It works is all we need to know." He pointed emphatically to the hole in his leg.

"The army's right," said MaryLou Krutch in disgust. "We been farting around too long. Why the hell don't you just take this damned thing, go up to that monster, and blow its guts out?"

The major hefted the alien weapon. "Ms. Krutch, I would be glad to give it a test firing. Would you mind showing the rest of us how it works?"

MaryLou sputtered, then pointed to the hole in Benny's leg.

"No," the major said. "I know what it does. I want to know how it does it."

Knobs, levers, buttons, depression, winking lights, slides, a low humming—all the ingredients were there.

"Shit," said MaryLou.

"Exactly," said the major.

"Give it here," said Kent, and accepted the artifact, held it close to his face, and shook his head in amazement.

"You seen that thing on TV or something, Lord?" Chita asked.

"Actually," he said, more to himself than to her, "it bears a remarkable resemblance to a secret weapon used by Robert the Bruce and the Black Douglas in their freedom battles against the King of . . ." He turned it over, studied it, sniffed it, whistled tunelessly. "Remarkable."

"Look," said Casopia, her voice rising in frustration, "we haven't got time to figure out how some damned thing or other from outer space works. I'm telling you, Nick had the answer. The only trouble was, he didn't have the right one. Specifically. Only theoretically."

Kent held the weapon close to his ear.

"Christ!" Casopia exploded. She looked toward the *Thing.* "We're going to die if we don't do something now!"

"We could leave," suggested Benny.

"Hey," said Ham Delphim and Milos Athnos simultaneously, and with such vehemence that each stared at the other with renewed respect. At the same time, MaryLou boxed his ears.

Casopia took the opportunity to explain as best she could the theory Nicodemus Hooker had explained to her. The others listened with increasing disdain, then subsiding scorn, then increasing interest.

Then the tank blew up.

And nothing stood between Gander Pond and the *Thing* except the backs of several dozen fleeing soldiers, a dozen or so remaining snipers, and Kent Montana, who slapped the Martian weapon heartily and said, "Major, I suggest you and these good people repair to some more protective area to work out your plan to stop this monster."

"Oh, really? And what are you going to do? Serve it tea and crumpets?"

"Watch your mouth!" Chita snarled.

"No," Kent said. "I am going to delay it. It won't be for very long, however, so please, do hurry."

The major continued to protest, but her men, the liberation army, and Casopia hustled her to the curb.

The thunder grew louder.

"You forgetting The Bomb, Lord?" Chita said.

Kent looked to the eastern horizon, or what was left of it, and the first smudged fingerprints of dawn that appeared above Gander Mountain. "No." He felt, for the first time in his life, a mote of pity for his mother. "No."

The *Thing* began a methodical sweep of the Jeeps that hadn't yet been melted into unrecognizable sludge. At the same time, it popped a few gaps in a few stores, blew out the rear wall of Marcello's, spiced up the kitchen of the Taco Supreme, and turned three of the snipers into shooting stars.

Debris pattered and slammed onto the street.

"You know," Chita said, "it looks like that dummy is moving in slow motion, you know what I mean?"

Kent did.

"Makes you wonder, don't it?"

He nodded.

"So," she said, "how you gonna work that thing?"

"Like this," Kent said. He adjusted a lever, slid a slide, thumbed a depression, and dialed a gauge. Then he pushed a button, and from its fan-shaped mouth shot a purple pulse ray not unlike the one that had dimpled Sister Lillian's wimple.

"Wow," Chita said.

The *Thing*, in turn, screamed, waved its non-weight-supporting appendages and possibly a pair of gossamer wings in wild agony, and sprayed its beams indiscriminately, with such an explosion of sound and fury that it seemed for a moment as if Kent had unnecessarily riled it.

Kent grinned.

He fired again.

The *Thing* thundered in an enraged frenzy, and some sort of liquid spurted from someplace in the region of what other aliens might have called its knees, if they had knees.

Chita cheered and slapped Kent's back.

However, Kent did not rejoice. He suspected that the weapon in hand had only a limited charge, and most certainly did not have the total stopping power he had counted on. A human would be drilled; the *Thing* was obviously only wounded. He just hoped he could stall the monster's inevitable march long enough for the major and the others to discover that which Nick Hooker had taken to his grave.

"Oh boy," said Chita in a low voice. "I think it ran out of cigarettes."

Kent frowned, then saw what she meant—the smoke and steam which had cocooned the *Thing* all this time had begun to dissipate, permitting more and more of its repulsive form to be exposed to the night. One of the last snipers shrieked in horror and threw himself from his roof. Several of the soldiers, who all had retreated to the columns and entrances of the four hotels, threw down their weapons and ran.

Phyllis Lager raced out of an alley, took one look at its indescribable being, and either fainted or was felled by a broken heart.

Chita shuddered and said, "Lord, this is major ugly here."

Kent fired.

The *Thing* roared, finally located the source of its torment, and glowered.

"Damn," Chita whispered. "It's got to be thirty feet tall, you know?"

"Oh, I wouldn't say that," Kent said. "Maybe nine or ten."

"Like hell."

"Indeed it is."

"I think we're in big trouble."

Kent was tired of making decisions that had nothing to do with camera angles and his good side. Nevertheless, he eased Chita aside with a gentle smile, hefted the alien weapon, and moved several yards toward the *Thing*, paying no attention to the woman's protests when she realized what his intentions were.

Mano a Thing, he thought grumpily, stopped, took a slow deep breath, and brought the alien's ray dispenser to his shoulder. He sensed there were but a few shots left. He had to make them count, or time would run out far quicker than he'd planned.

"In for a penny," he said, and prepared to fire.

"Swell," he heard Chita mutter then. "Famous last words."

As good as any, he thought.

Froze.

Listened to the increasing thunder.

Widened his eyes.

Turned slowly and said to her, "I've got it!"

She pointed. "Not yet. But soon."

Shaking his head, unable to stop grinning, he ran over to her and took hold of her arm. "I know why Nick failed," he said gleefully. "Damn, you're good." He kissed her. Kissed her again. Looked over his shoulder and kissed her a third time. "Now listen," he said urgently, "tell the major, now, how Nick went wrong. But hurry! I've not much power left in this, I think."

She grinned.

She ran.

She ran back. "How?"

He told her.

She grinned.

She kissed him.

She ran.

Kent strode back to his position and met what he assumed was the *Thing*'s gaze without flinching.

There was nothing but rubble, wreckage, and ruin left in the street.

The *Thing* casually clawed aside a Jeep and faced him squarely.

All firing stopped.

A woman hustled her weeping child across the street and out of the way.

One of the soldiers played a mournful tune on a harmonica.

The wind gusted out of the black sky, scattering paper and dust across the bleak blacktop.

A tumbleweed bounced and quivered along the gutter.

Slowly the *Thing* raised its head.

Slowly Kent brought the weapon back to his shoulder.

For nearly a full minute they faced each other, measuring each other, examining each other for signs of vulnerability.

It snorted like a bull just before the onset of its charge.

Kent wiped a rush of perspiration from his brow.

It fired a quick burst far above Kent's head, but he would have none of it. He wasn't about to waste the last of his energy ammunition on such a transparent diversion.

It snorted again.

He wished someone would call to him from the sidelines and tell him to get the hell out of the street, he was only a butler, for crying out loud, and besides, they'd found someone old enough to remember what he had told Chita.

The thunder reached a crescendo that caused the creature to straighten in clear perplexity.

Lowering the weapon, though not distracting his aim, Kent dared a glance over his shoulder and nearly wept in relief. There, thundering down the center of Main Street, was Artie Chong, riding a proud palomino at the head of a full troop of the U.S. government's finest secret cavalry. Steam poured from the horses' nostrils, their manes tossed in the wind, and their hooves beat a tattoo on the blacktop that soon had the street full again of the down but not out citizens of Gander Pond.

Sophia ran out from one of the hotels and tried to drag Artie from the saddle.

Bitinia Player shoved her aside and tried to drag Artie from the saddle that belonged to her brother.

The major ran out, shoved Bit aside, and snapped an order to the chef. Artie frowned, looked toward Kent, who nodded vigorously, then turned and passed on the instructions to the rest of his men.

Kent rolled his shoulders, felt tension fall to the ground as the leaves in autumn, and actually managed a lopsided smile for the creature that looked less puzzled now than downright apprehensive.

It knows, he thought; damn, the critter knows it's beaten.

It snorted.

He heard people moving stealthily then, slipping out of the streets to the blocks behind Main; he heard the cavalry animals shaking their bits; he heard footsteps stop just behind him and felt a hand touch his back. Softly.

"I'm with you, Lord," Chita whispered.

"Baron," he corrected with a wistful smile.

"Whatever."

He nodded *why not?* and noted with a shiver of alarm that the sky above Gander Mountain was much lighter than it had been just a few minutes before. He caught himself straining to hear the engines of a jet or a bomber, the harbinger of the last scene he would ever play in his life.

"Are they ready?"

No immediate answer.

The *Thing* grumbled, rumbled, then took a step toward him.

Kent took a step toward it.

"Are they ready?"

It took another step.

Kent took another step.

"Jesus, Chita."

Closer.

Louder.

Closer.

Louder.

A finger touched his shoulder.

"Ready," she whispered.

Kent nodded. He was ready; he wasn't ready. He was terrified; he was beyond terror. He was sweating; his throat was desert dry. His heels were loud; his heart was louder.

What the hell, he thought.

"Scots wha' hae," he said proudly, and fired.

"Charge!" Artie Chong bellowed behind him.

"Charge!" Major Settbach bellowed from the shadows.

The *Thing* said not a word.

It only charged.

The final assault appeared at first blush to be chaotic, appeared at first glance to be the last desperate attempt of a few dozen human beings against an all-powerful denizen of the fourth planet from the sun.

Yet Kent immediately saw a method of this nonsense, and as he strode unhurriedly toward the creature, firing from the hip, he knew that his part was just as crucial as any other.

He struck the monster on one of its shoulders; it slapped helplessly at the wound and turned, just in time to come face-or-something-to-face with a half dozen people on a rooftop screaming, "Aw, Lassie," and laughing.

He tore a ragged gouge in its side, causing it to spin the other way and meet a farewell to Mrs. Calabash, wherever she was.

He nicked its knee, and it staggered backward, turned, and saw dozens of courageous, giggling schoolchildren throwing it kisses from their palms, thanking it for coming, and laughing.

It fought back.

It burned the tops of every tree left within five blocks; it toppled the newspaper office in a fiery blast of stone and ink and flaming paper; it picked off several verbal snipers one by one, with both ray and paw, to send them screaming to their deaths on the hard concrete below; it caught a trio of soldiers in a doorway, trying to remember how the hell Milton Berle ended his show, remembering too late as their families became instant dependents.

But there was too much.

Artie and the cavalry rode around it, singing "Happy Trails to You" at the top of their collective, well-modulated, and hastily harmonized voices. It spun away from them dizzily, striking out and roaring, catching a few with its crimson and ocher and decidedly off-color rays, missing too many more as they raced unerringly into the second verse and chorus.

The schoolchildren, faces scratched and burned and freckled with fear, their clothing shredded and their socks rolled down, shrieked, "Because we like you!" as they laughed and applauded and picked up their fallen comrades.

And still Kent fired.

The top of the Holy Tabernacle Society Today Tabernacle blew off in a tornado of shattered neon and wood.

And still Kent fired.

The windows of the Greenland Glen's top floor blew out; the lobby of the Mountain Resort took a direct, explosive hit.

Kent fired.

There was laughing.

There was applause.

And suddenly . . . there was silence.

The *Thing* and Kent Montana were only ten feet apart.

The top arc of the morning sun had begun to rise above the mountain.

The distant roar of a bomber could be heard in the west.

Fire crackled and smoke filled the air once again; buildings sagged, a lamppost crumbled, tree split open as if struck by lightning.

Oh boy, Kent thought as the *Thing* slowly lowered its head and eyed him carefully.

"Take it easy, Lord," Chita said. "Break a leg."

She ran.

The *Thing* ignored her.

She ran back and put her arms around Kent's waist.

"You came back," he said.

She grinned. "It's traditional."

If I'm wrong, he thought, it's all over but the frying.

It seemed to smile sardonically at him, seemed to tell him that it admired him for figuring out its weakness, but figuring it out too late because it still had one ace up its sleeve, one shot in the chamber, one arrow in the quiver.

It set a display of ray and heat and beam power over Kent's and Chita's heads.

It was laughing.

Kent scowled.

It breathed.

Chita nearly swooned.

It said, smugly, "Say goodnight, Gracie."

And Kent Montana answered, "Goodnight, Gracie."

It choked.

It gasped.

It began to smoke from various visible and recessed orifices, steam from the cuts and lacerations and holes in its hide, hiss from those orifices that permitted hissing and steaming and foul-smelling smoking.

It trembled.

Kent backed Chita away.

It threw whatever the hell it called its arms and other appendages toward the rising sun.

And it screamed.

It roared.

It bellowed.

It blew up.

· 5 ·

"Boy," said Chita Juarel as she sat with Kent on the curb opposite the Pagoda. "Two lousy words. Can you beat it? Hooker missed by two lousy words."

Kent, exhausted, merely grunted and watched the dazed citizens of Gander Pond set about the arduous task of cleaning up and rebuilding their town. It was difficult to think, and so he didn't. Instead, he let the fresh light of the new day warm him as he noted the parade of humanity unfold before him.

Sophia Chong stood across the street with Artie, in front of the wreckage of their restaurant.

"You never told me you could ride a horse," she scolded with tears of gratitude in her eyes.

"I cannot lie, my dragon of the pasta supreme," he said with downcast modesty. "They tied me on."

"They didn't!"

"They did."

She hugged him. "Lord, I love you, Arthur."

He looked at the still scantily clad but definitely chastened Sordette Biletto over his wife's shoulder. "And I shall never stray from the path of my chosen profession again. From this day forward, my darling dumpling, I shall wok the wok and forgo the talk."

"Liar," she whispered lovingly.

Artie Chong only winked.

Kent grinned and looked up the street.

Horace O'Malley stood with his daughter and Sergeant Fabian Lamanza in front of the wreckage of the newspaper office.

"Kitty, can you ever forgive me for putting the story ahead of your safety?"

Kitty smiled through her tears. "You've got the exclusive, right?"

O'Malley nodded.

"Then I guess we'll get rich and move out of this town."

The editor perked up. "Say, daughter, you could be right, at that."

"And when Fabian is on leave, he can come visit?"

Sergeant Lamanza shrugged sheepishly. His hair was a mess.

"Like hell," said O'Malley. "If we're going to be rich, you can do better than that."

Kitty looked shocked. "Father!"

"Think about it," he counseled.

"Okay," she said.

Kent shook his head at the way some people reacted to tragedy, and watched as Phyllis Lager worked the streets with a tambourine in one hand, a Bible in the other. She had already tried to solicit funds from him for the rebuilding of her Tabernacle and a three-story headstone for Sister Lillian's grave, but he had no money. None. He was broke.

The secret government cavalry had already left before the light had grown too strong and the people too alert to recall what they had seen. She had stopped her black stallion in front of him and had given him a smart salute.

"You're quite a man, Mr. Montana," she'd complimented.

"Bug off," growled Chita.

"Thank you," Kent had answered gallantly. "I must say, I've never quite met anyone like you, either."

The major had blushed.

Sergeant Delphim, on a horse beside her, had said, "Major, it's getting late."

"Sure thing, Hammy," she'd answered, winked at Kent's astonishment, and led the troop quickly and secretively out of town.

Time passed.

Frazzled and weary doctors made the rounds of those involved in the final battle, tending to wounds, seeing to the dead and dying, and giving comfort to those who worried about their insurance.

He saw Benny Hart get arrested for attempting to liberate whatever he could carry from whatever store still had its display windows shattered.

He saw MaryLou Krutch, her pheasant feather a little bedraggled, hoist a backpack to her shoulders and trudge out of town.

Mayor James Ellader took forty-two rolls of pictures.

And finally, as the outside world became aware of what had happened in this small New Jersey town, he saw a spiffy red motor scooter wend its way through the destruction, its driver wearing western boots, jeans, a denim jacket, and a weathered grey western hat.

He stopped in front of Kent.

"You Kent Montana?" he asked. He was bearded, with long brown hair, a fairly but not unreasonably prominent nose, and he wore a bat ring on his left hand.

Kent looked to Chita, looked to the rider, and nodded.

The rider reached into a large compartment over the scooter's rear wheel, pulled out a fat manila envelope, and handed it to him.

"What's this?" Kent asked.

The messenger smiled. "The script for your next picture."

Kent couldn't believe it. "My . . . god. Are you sure?"

The messenger kicked his machine into motion and called over his shoulder, "Pal, if I don't know, nobody does."

"Well, I'll be damned," Kent said, hefting the package lovingly.

Chita cleared her throat.

He looked at her, looked at the package, and said, "Well, I guess I won't starve, anyway."

"Nope."

He opened it, glanced at the first page, and smiled. "It seems as if it takes place in England."

"Ah."

He glanced at the street. "Have you ever been to England?"

She stood and stretched.

He stood and stretched.

They walked down the center of the street. Silently. Hand in hand. Until Gander Pond was well behind them.

To either side of them, the forest that hadn't been destroyed by the Martian invader was alive with the songs of birds and the rustlings of little things that hid behind the trees.

They passed the ruins of the Gander Palace.

"You tired?" he asked.

"Nope," she said.

They walked to Gander Mountain and stood for a moment at the place where the Jersey cowboy had lost his life.

They gazed at the remains of the Tabernacle limousine.

They exchanged glances of an unknown nature and took a well-defined trail to the mountain's summit. There they found what was left of the spacecraft the creature had taken to Earth.

"Amazing," he said.

"I ain't going to England."

He wasn't surprised. "I know."

"I think I'll go back to Atlantic City."

"I guessed as much."

She slipped into his arms. "Not for a while, though."

He smiled. "That's all right with me."

They kissed.

And the sun rose higher.

The spaceship lost its glow.

But in a lonely hollow at the back of the crater, there was a faint purple light that pulsed and shimmered.

And when the sunlight struck it fully, there was no doubt it was a nest.

A Martian nest.

Filled with eggs.

–V–

Epilogue

Kent Montana, delighted that Chita Juarel was every bit as soft and wonderful as he had dreamed, gently disengaged his embrace.

"What's the matter?" she asked. "You don't want to fool around?"

"Indeed, I very much want to fool around," he said.

"Well, then, what's the problem, Lord?"

Kent winked at her and climbed into the crater, climbed over the remains of the spaceship, and found the little hollow where the eggs of the Martian invader lay.

He looked at them, looked up, and said, "Forget it."

And crushed them, one by one.

THE CREDITS

STARRING AS THEMSELVES:

Cpl. Milos Athnos
Sordette Biletto
Arthur Chong
Sophia Chong
Pfc. Ham Delphim
Eunice Ellader
Mayor James Ellader
Janis Ellader
Casopia Gumpers
Benny Hart
Dr. Nicodemus Hooker
Chita Juarel
MaryLou Krutch

Rev. Phil Lager
Rev. Phyllis Lager
Pvt. Fabian Lamanza
Kent Montana
Horace O'Malley
Kitty O'Malley
Bitinia Player
Extra Player
Maj. Wendy Settbach
John Smith
Officer Lucian Twiller
Sister Lillian Vorth
M. Sgt. Porter Wagoneer

SPECIAL APPEARANCES BY:

Old lady driver............................Old Alice
Blackthorne ....Lincoln Blackthorne
Portly old man.............................Macon Crowley
Sleeping old man ....Palmer Crowley
Script messenger..........................Mysterious Person

And:

SPARKY THE ADEQUATE DOG

Producer ....AT&T 6300HD (free plug)
Director...Lionel Fenn
Writer ....Lionel Fenn
Editor ....Ginjer Buchanan
Technical Assistance (jokes) .... Craig Shaw Gardner
Technical Assistance (U.S. Army) .... Dan Quayle
Special Effects ....God
Costumes ....Lincoln Blackthorne
Catering........................Friday Wong's House of Chili
Best Boy ....Randy Savage
Best Girl .... Meg Tilley
Carpenter .... John
Music Composed and Arranged by ... Nobody you ever heard of
Main Titles ....AST TurboLaser (another free plug)
Director's Brother ....Geoffrey Marsh
Director's Other Brother....................... Timothy Boggs
Assistant to the Director .... Felicia Andrews (deceased)
Assistant to the Producer......Jersey Central Power & Light

AND SPECIAL THANKS TO:

Elisabeth Roberts, who decided we shouldn't use the vomit
jokes; the Kent Montana Fan Club; and the Gander Pond
Urban Renewal Commission, James Ellader, Director, without whose help this project wouldn't have had anything to
blow up.

THE FINEST THE UNIVERSE HAS TO OFFER